IN THE CUT

A COLLECTION OF SHORT STORIES

MICHAEL LOCKETT

CATAMOUNT
PRESS

an imprint of Sunbury Press, Inc.
Mechanicsburg, PA USA

CATAMOUNT
PRESS

an imprint of Sunbury Press, Inc.
Mechanicsburg, PA USA

For information about special discounts for bulk purchases, please contact Sunbury Press Orders Dept. at (855) 338-8359 or orders@sunburypress.com.

To request one of our authors for speaking engagements or book signings, please contact Sunbury Press Publicity Dept. at publicity@sunburypress.com.

FIRST CATAMOUNT PRESS EDITION: September 2023

Set in Adobe Garamond | Interior design by Crystal Devine | Cover by Lawrence Knorr | Edited by Taylor Berger-Knorr.

Publisher's Cataloging-in-Publication Data
Names: Lockett, Michael, author.
Title: In the cut : a collection of short stories / Michael Lockett.
Description: First trade paperback edition. | Mechanicsburg, PA : Catamount Press, 2023.
Summary: Life in Appalachia is like a kid standing in the center of a seesaw. It's a fragile balance, somewhere between the old world and the new, flat-broke or getting by, rooted in place or getting out. If the seesaw comes down hard, it knocks folks right off. Think laid off miners, gravediggers, dishwashers, Mennonite farmers, and Wal-Mart cashiers. Folks In the Cut live somewhere between the balance and the fall.
Identifiers: ISBN : 979-8-88819-061-6 (softcover) | ISBN : 979-8-88819-062-3 (ePub).
Subjects: FICTION / Literary.

Product of the United States of America
0 1 1 2 3 5 8 13 21 34 55

For the Love of Books!

To the human commodity living day to day in the spoils of capitalism. We deserve to be set loose on paper too.

CONTENTS

VII   Acknowledgments

1   The Blast

10   More Than an Accident

15   After the Hunter

30   Under the Table

36   Lisa Frank Cosmos

47   Unspoken

51   Neighbor Boys

60   A Son Without Compassion

76   We Bury Our Own

91   A Good Father

99   Gallows' Hill

127   About the Author

ACKNOWLEDGMENTS

I'd like to thank my Pap and Gram Philips. She, a legacy of love. He, a legacy of hard work. I like to thank my mom, who is infinitely kind. After dad left, she raised five kids on her own with nothing in a little old house. She picked frozen coal from the pile in the yard for our pot belly stove to keep us warm. She commanded an arsenal of buckets to catch rainwater from the endless leaks in the roof to keep us dry. She heated water on a gas burner to bathe us in a rinse tub and sent us out into the world well-fed, in nice clothes, and with the belief that we were loved and no less than anyone else. To the crazy Lockett family, the Kneppy tribe, and the Philips brood. This one's for you! To my brothers, Davey, Eric, and Matt and my sister Missy. I love you. To my friends here in Pittsburgh, the old Pegasus crew, I am forever grateful for you. To my partner, Christopher, to your love and our home. To my wonderful cats and crazy birds. Wouldn't the world be wonderful if humans were even half as good as you are?

I'd like to thank the amazing community of writers at Carlow University: Tess Barry, Dr. Lou Boyle, and Jan Beatty. I'd like to thank my brilliant mentors, Geeta Kothari, Karin Lin-Greenberg, and Carlow Gebler. They are masters of this hard, hard craft. Please, read their work. I'd like to thank Sunbury Press for giving me a shot and my editor Taylor Berger-Knorr for the grueling work of combing over these prose.

THE BLAST

Coal Run, Pennsylvania. July of '84, the day of the blast. Mom had shut all the windows first thing when she got up at five a.m. The air was sweltering. I woke with the violent feeling of a hot, hard sleep. I checked, first thing, to see if I'd gotten my period. Nothing yet. The fear of getting knocked-up by Jessie Mason before my junior year of high school washed over me. Worse yet, the *I-messed-up-big-time* talk with Daddy and Mom sat like a pit in the gut. I pulled off my sweaty bedding and threw it in the hamper. I put on my clothes from the day before: overall shorts and a faded pink T-shirt. No use wasting clean on the day.

I went down the hall of our little two-bedroom place. It was just the same as all the others in the holler, built for the old company mine. There were about five clapboard shotgun houses spaced a half-acre apart on either side of the gravel road. The road was lined with sycamore trees that had grown giant over the years and dwarfed the houses. The trees constantly shed their bark, which filled the ditches and blew like bits of old brown paper down the road.

I pulled my hair into a ponytail as I stepped into our little kitchen. The morning sun beamed through the window above the sink. The clock on the wall softly ticked just past seven. The back door was still open to catch the bit of air through the screen door. A slew of sterilized canning jars sat spotless on the counter, reflecting the sun. Five pies lined the cooling rack next to the stove. The blueberry-stained crust peeked out over the edges of tea towels. A horsefly milled about the cloth. The sweet smell owned the room, but the heat in the air and my worry—some big idea of cravings, put me right off them.

I looked for a trace of Daddy. No mining helmet. No lunch pail near the door. No work boots beneath the coal stain on the wall where he leaned his rear day-in, day-out to take them off. There'd been talk of layoffs at the old underground mines, for which our little hamlet was built. Everyone knew they sold the rights to the strip-mining outfit from Syracuse. I remembered Daddy saying at dinner the night before though, "They'll have us tunneling coal till they anchor that last stick of dynamite in that bedrock on the mountain top." Seemed he was right.

I started to clear the mess of baking sheets soaking in the sink. I scraped my fingernail over the burned spill-over of berry juice on the tin.

I saw Mom through the window. She was hunched over in our large garden in her old herringbone dress. The garden nearly took up the entire yard. She picked through tomatoes, filled the old wooden bins she used for gathering. "Why don't you wear slacks around the house, at least?" I'd asked her time and again. However, she said, being raised Pentecost, to dress holiness, she'd never feel right to go around in slacks. Yet her skirt arched above her calves when she stooped.

"Bett," Mom called for me from the garden.

"Coming," I said as I dried my hands on the sides of my shorts.

The wooden screen door off the kitchen clapped at my heels as I headed onto the back porch.

Our house was on a high elevation. From the back porch, I looked toward the foot of the holler where the mountain peaks in half a mile's distance stood tall. They'd stripped out the trees on the peaks. They stood like bald, brown caps of sand, rock, and slate. They looked like something from TV out West rising from the plains. But here, they were an unnatural thing that defied the thicket of green over the rolling hills. Not far from the peaks, a towering dragline struck the air like a pin in a cushion. In the distance, I could hear the beeps of the backhoes and loaders of the strip mine crushing over the trees. The trees made a ripping sound at the root and something akin to a groan when they fell.

"Bett," Mom called again.

"I'm coming," I said and went for the garden.

In the garden, Mom's hands moved quickly from one tomato to the next.

"I can't believe Daddy had work today," I said. "Why wouldn't they just let 'em go? Everyone knows the underground works sold off."

"He was going to boycott but grew weary. Couldn't sign up if it looked like he quit," Mom said. She stood up, put her hands on her waist. She coughed with her fist over her mouth, and her pudgy belly gave a jerk at the front of her dress. She lifted her collar and wiped the sweat from her neck. Her thick, curly hair, pulled back in a bun, rose around her head in a frizz. She pointed me to the bin full of tomatoes for me to take back to the house.

"The other women should be here soon for canning," she said.

I stepped to the bin piled high with ripe, red tomatoes at the edge of the garden. I anchored my legs on either side of it. I hoisted it up onto my right shoulder.

Mom wiped her brow with the back of her arm. She put her hand above her hip the way she did when it ached. Then, she stooped at the vines. "I reckon the blast could go off any time. Shut the door when you get back to the house or everything we own will be covered in dust," she said.

"Yes, ma'am," I said.

Already, I felt the sweat bead on my neck. The gnats were thick over the garden, and one flew into my eye. I used my free hand to wipe it from the flesh of my lower eyelid.

A swell of the periodical cicadas that had emerged that summer buzzed in the woods around the yard and flitted through the treetops. There were spots of naked branches in the thicket where they'd already been taken bare, and their pervasive crunching could be heard through the brush.

"I don't know what's worse, the strip-mine or those cicadas," I said.

"It'll be a fine day when both are gone," Mom said.

"Every move I make, I anticipate a big boom," I said.

Mom raised her brow and gave a nod as she moved her hands from one tomato to the next. She skipped over one. Its skin had burst with what looked like a sore of white pus.

"Something," Mom said. "Some grow juicy, ripe-red. Some stay green, get worm-rot and gnarly. Others overripen, dead on the vine."

"Something," I said as I turned with the bin, not quite sure what she was getting at. Again, I made eyes for the bald hills and the dragline.

Our neighbors, Ms. Georgie and Mrs. Mason, walked together across the yards toward the house. Each carried a bin of tomatoes fit to can. Little Everly, Mrs. Mason's youngest, around eight or so, ran around them. She spun across the yard. Her shiny bobbed hair bounced as she whirled. The cloth belt attached to her terry cloth dress dragged behind her on either side. Her shoulder fell out of the dress, which was unzipped in the back, like she'd just thrown it on.

Everly raced for me. She threw her arms at my waist. Nearly knocked me down.

"Easy," I said and gently wrapped Everly on her head with my free hand.

She looked up at me with her wild, big eyes. "Still no blast," Everly said. She opened her mouth long and wide, showing off a big, pink wad of gum.

"Breakfast of champions," I said.

"I got pockets full," Everly said. She stepped back and opened the bulging pockets of her dress for a good look inside. There she had several pieces of Bazooka gum. Everly stuck her tongue in the middle of the wad in her mouth to blow a bubble, but when she blew, instead, she nearly spit it out.

"Mind yourself. You're liable to choke," I said. Yet, I expected Everly wouldn't listen. There was something in Everly set on doing the opposite of everything she was told.

Everly ran steps ahead of me onto the porch. She swung around with her hand on the post. As she did this, the crazed green paint flakes peeled off like eggshells at Everly's touch.

"Morning, Ms. Georgie. Mrs. Mason," I said, as the women came close.

I stepped with the woman onto the porch. The floor slats sagged, what I imagined like planks on an old ship deck, worn slick from the steps to the door, and our feet made a clunking sound as we walked across them.

We put our bins together near the screen door.

I pulled the door shut, just as Mom had asked. "Hold still," I said to Everly, and I grabbed her by the loose ends of her belt. I tied the belt. Then I zipped up the back of her dress.

We all looked toward the bald hills.

"Ought to blast it up their rears," Ms. Georgie said.

I laughed at her words, the comical sight of her wrinkly face beneath her thinning gray hair which was pinned tight with bobby pins and showed her white scalp.

"They'll strip us out to our front doors," Mrs. Mason said. "Mark my word. They'll take this place down to clay. Rust-red water that'll stink of sulfur, not fit for drink nor wash." A look of worry washed over her bright eyes. Her straight, graying roots showed an inch in contrast with her auburn permed hair. She always stood hunched a bit with her hips forward. She folded her arms at her waist.

"Has Jessie gone off to the mines with Jude?" I asked Mrs. Mason.

"Why wouldn't he?" she asked. She turned to me with a straight look in her eyes, like, *When did you become so interested in what Jessie does?* All the tough union talk on strikes going around, everyone having an opinion, I reckoned maybe Mrs. Mason mistook me. I wasn't calling Jessie a scab. *God forbid. Had she caught wind we fooled around?*

Well, he's getting laid off, and I might be his baby's mom, I thought. But I shrugged, bit my lip. I could feel the shame sweep over my eyes. "Daddy's gone," I said to clear the air. *We* were no better, after all.

Just then, Mom came onto the porch behind us. She sat another bin full down with the rest. "I'd say we had a good crop."

"Lord provides," Ms. Georgie said. She raised her brow. The creases folded over her forehead.

"Mushroom soil helps," Mom said, looking proudly over her bins.

"When they blast that mountain top, it'll be like a volcano going off," Everly said. She stood surprisingly still with her arms folded tight, her eyes fast on the bald mountain caps. "I saw a volcano on a reel at school. Red hot lava comes out the top. Flows like a river and burns up everything in its path."

"You think so?" Mom asked Everly. "We'll see what happens, I guess," she said.

Challenged, I reckon, Everly spun off the porch, still chomping her gum.

"Girl, you fall, you'll choke," Mrs. Mason said. "You were told to take a piece at a time. Not hog it all at once."

Everly kept spinning. She jutted further into the yard away from us, shaking her head and crunching her face, mocking her mom.

Mrs. Mason put her hands on her hips and furrowed her brow.

Ms. Georgie shook her head and huffed. It embodied everything she said when Mrs. Mason wasn't around. *That little brat Everly needed a good, hard swat.*

Just then, Jude Mason, Daddy, and Jessie came through the edge of the yard from the footpaths to the old mines in the woods, still in their miners' caps. They looked more beast than man, all covered in soot. The whites of their eyes were taken red as they often were from the coal dust. They looked frightful, even from afar.

"It's official," Mom said, with her eyes fast on the men.

As the men passed the garden, passed whirling Everly, they looked hard through the trees for a good look at the mountains. Their boots clunked at the planks as they joined us on the porch where we all packed together.

Daddy pushed in close to me. His eyes were intent on the blast. Soot sat deep in his pores in specks of black and lined the fine wrinkle of his skin like dark little streams.

"Isn't that progress," Jude Mason said.

Daddy riffled through his pocket, fetched his chew, and fingered the pink slip over his Copenhagen can. He handed the slip to Mom. He turned the lid of his chew, scooped his finger in, and dipped a wad in his mouth.

"What did you get on your report card?" Mom asked. She unfolded the half-slip of paper.

"Nothing," Daddy said. "I got expelled." He rolled his tongue over the skin of his lower jaw to pack in his snuff.

"That's a framer," Mrs. Mason said, as she gathered up Jude's slip.

"Twenty-four years, for what?" Jude asked.

For the first time since we messed around, I laid hard eyes on Jessie. He lit a smoke with his hand cupped around his lighter flame.

"That is a bon-e-fied pink slip if I ever saw one," Jessie said inhaling. He breathed out a big puff. He put his lighter back in his pocket with his cigarette pack and pulled his slip out. He handed it to his mom.

Regret was all I knew of Jessie. *What came over me that day?* I was over at the Mason's babysitting Everly, and there he was. When I left, he walked me back on the trails looking for raspberries, he said. He offered me a cigarette. I took it. We lounged in the ferns, inching closer to one another beneath our clouds of smoke. I never thought things would go as far as they did. Full-on. Jessie had a boyish face and a wild head of blond curls. Guess it got the best of me. He wasn't bright though or manly, fit to marry. He was more the kind of guy I figured would be nothing but a headache, made me imagine waiting up lonely nights nursing a baby with no food in the house. Nothing to swallow down but regret to say Jesse was the baby's dad.

When Jessie caught eyes with me, he glanced away fast. I reckoned from his reaction; he was just as regretful as I was.

"You'll need that, if you're planning on signing up," Mrs. Mason said. She reached for Jessie's pink slip and folded it together with his dad's. She reached into the top of her shirt and tucked them in her bra.

Everly ran toward us, crashed into us like a bowling ball into pins.

"Give me that gum," Daddy said, and he stomped hard against the planks of the porch. He leaned into Everly, like he was ready to square off.

"No way," Everly said. She balled up her fist and shook it at Daddy.

Daddy growled playfully at her, something between a snort and a snarl.

Everly squealed. She spun around my legs.

"Settle," Mom said, teasing Dad. "What you fixin' on doing with a day off? I got about eight bushel of green beans needs pickin'," Mom said. Then, she gave dad a good finger jab to the rib.

"Well, I was fixin' to go snoop around that strip mining outfit over there," Daddy said.

"Why don't you go ask them for a job?" Mom said.

"What do you think a big-time operation would want with a hill-jack?" Daddy asked. Daddy sneered at Mom. "Isn't she something, your mother? I might go back, volunteer at the defunct mine," Daddy said. Then he looked at me and smiled. He took off his helmet, bent down with a groan, and sat on the edge of the porch facing the blast.

Just a look at him, the fatigue, the way his shoulders fell like it was the first he'd sat down in years, was enough to make me cry with shame, thinking what I'd done with Jessie. How would I ever get up the courage to tell if I was—

I put my hands in Daddy's sweaty, wet hair. He looked up at me. I gave Daddy a weak smile and looked away fast.

Over the furthest bald mountain, a BOOM shot out. The reverberation flashed through the body in a wave. A flock of birds scattered from the trees in the woods. They cawed as they flapped across the sky. The cicadas swarmed from the forest treetops like little specks in the shape of clouds. BOOM! Another blast shot off. Then a third. There were five blasts that rumbled like thunder with dirt that rose in smoke like brown, rolling stacks.

"Everly! Everly!" I heard Mrs. Mason cry out.

Amidst the sound of the blast, I looked to Everly to find her cheeks full, her eyes wide and round, her arms flailing in the air.

Mrs. Mason swatted Everly on the back. "God, she's choking!" Mrs. Mason cried out.

Jessie snatched Everly up. He put his forearms under her ribs and gave a big thrust. Everly spit out the gum with a cough, started bawling right away, and pressed her face into Jessie's neck.

"I told her, goddamn it! I told her!" Mrs. Mason said.

We clamored on the porch, fussed over Everly, while the blasts continued on the mountain tops. The stacks of smoke and ash dispersed like inkblots in the sky.

I felt the slight taste of earth in my mouth as the dust settled over us. I felt a flush come over me and a terrible ache in my gut.

From the haze in the air, a mass of cicadas swept the sky from the direction of the blast. They settled over our yard with their loud buzz, like an end-time plague. We looked on in awe as some dropped from the sky into the grass.

Everly still squalled to my back. I turned to look at Jessie, who held her tight, still, against him. *Maybe I'm wrong?* I thought. *Maybe, Jessie ain't so bad?*

"You're bleeding," Daddy said, turned from his seat on the edge of the porch, his head near my thigh.

He swiped his finger over the stream of blood dripping toward my knee.

I jumped back, thought fast. "Everly," I said. "Caught me with her nail."

I turned for the door, pushed past Jessie and Everly. God, the smell of him, the Brute, cigarette smoke and coal dust, was enough to make me want to puke.

"Bett," Mom said, as I went into the house. "Put on a pot of coffee. We'll cut into one of those pies."

"OK," I said. "After I tend to this cut."

I blotted the blood from my groin in the bathroom as I dry-heaved, bent over, felt near ready to die. I heard more BOOMS from inside the house. The walls rattled as the earth quaked with each one.

I swear, the blast took it from me. This was what I wanted after all. But, at what felt like the end the world, the loss tore me up same as the blast on the mountain top.

MORE THAN AN ACCIDENT

I stood in the back of the funeral parlor next to Great Uncle Walter. I looked away to avoid the photo of the accident in his hand. I'd already seen it three times, though Mom told me not to look, and I feared I'd be caught sneaking another peek. Cold air came from the vents in the ceiling. Sad hymns played in the room.

There were around twenty people there. Two stood at Uncle Butch's urn. Two greeted my father and grandparents who sat in the front row. Some, like my mom and Ms. Lorraine, sat talking in the back rows of chairs. Others stood, whispering in the corners of the room.

Beside Uncle Butch's urn, there were blue flowers Mom called carnations spread out like peacock feathers. Their strange smell filled the room. They didn't smell sweet and rosy like the ones in the yard, but more like powder and the air in the freezer at home.

When I turned back to Uncle Walter, he stood with his magnifying glass, showing some man the photo of Uncle Butch's crash. I looked toward Mom to be sure she wasn't watching me. I looked again at the photo. The charred-out cab of Uncle Butch's truck was turned around on the railroad tracks. The engine of the train was stuck into its side.

Walter put the magnifying glass close to the photo to show the man Butch's skull, which could be seen through the dark cab in the driver's seat of the truck.

The man let out a gasp.

"The train dragged the truck some five-hundred-feet. The explosion knocked the engine from the track," Walter said.

I noticed Mom turn. She gave me a come-here curl of the finger, so I went to her through an aisle of chairs. I expected she'd scold me for looking at the picture again.

"Sit here," she said.

I sat in the cold, metal folding chair beside her.

Ms. Lorraine was turned in her seat in the aisle in front of us. "How old are you?" she asked me. She pinched the corner of her rose-tinted glasses with her finger and her thumb and looked me over.

"Nine," I said.

"And aren't you a picture of Uncle Butch and your dad when they were boys," Ms. Lorraine said. "I should know. I babysat them. Didn't they give me a hard time. You don't do that to your mom?" She asked.

"No, ma'am," I said.

My dad sat just ahead of us next to my grandparents. The back of his arm rested on the empty chair beside him, in view of Butch's urn. I looked past Dad's curled up fist to the urn.

Seeing the urn, I couldn't help but wonder—

"How'd they fit Butch into such a small thing?" I asked Mom.

"They turned his bones into ashes, like a powder," she said.

"Is his spirit in there?" I asked.

"Oh no. The spirit goes back to God who gave it," Mom said.

"Oh," I said.

"What do you remember most about your uncle?" Miss Lorraine asked me. Her face moved into my view, like the moon into the night sky. I caught the old-lady perfume of her and the Lifesaver breath mint that rolled in her tongue when she spoke. Her eyes tightened, and crow's feet filled the corners of them when she forced a smile.

"His goat Lucifer," I said.

"A billy goat!" she said. "Named Lucifer!" Then, she puffed her shoulders, drew her head back, and shook it. "That Butch! That's a bad thing to do, name a goat after the Devil."

"You had about thirty seconds to get from the car to Butch's trailer door before Lucifer was bucking at your rear," Mom said. "That goat and Butch were a lot alike."

Just about then, Old Aunt May came through the door and caught my eye. She wore a long black dress and a hair covering on her head. She stopped at the urn and put her hand on it. She stood there for a while, then turned to my grandparents and my dad with a hanky under her nose.

"Aunt May. The old-time Pentecost," Ms. Lorraine said.

"Folks don't dress holiness like that anymore," Mom said.

Aunt May joined hands with my dad and grandparents. She prayed in tongues and swayed. Her teeth chattered and her head quivered. The prayer grew to a wail that hurt my ear.

I pressed my head into my mom, and she put her arm around me.

"Don't fear the Holy Spirit," Mom whispered. Then, she kissed me on the head.

My father raised his arm in the air. "Bless the Lord," he said. Then he started to pray in tongues too. His always sounded something like, "Kashunda-ka-book-kashunda—" And he said this over and over again.

Dad was a minister. Uncle Butch always called him Reverend Ike, after the preacher on the radio. Mom said this wasn't nice because Reverend Ike was a crook.

After the prayer died down, a hush fell over the room.

I thought more about Miss Lorraine's question.

I remembered most the day we were visiting Uncle Butch's trailer. While my dad was in the yard, Butch asked Mom why she had bruises on her neck. Butch went outside. I watched from the screen door, as he raised his fist to my dad like a prizefighter. "I'll teach you to cuff up your wife," he said. Then, Uncle Butch and my dad went rounds. Lucifer sprinted around them making his terrible maa-maa sound. Uncle Butch gave my dad a bloody nose.

"Butch was always up to some trouble," Miss Lorraine said. "I was at that tent revival, up Moss Creek, and Butch was cutting up in his seat. Reverend Hugill stopped preaching and called him out in front of everyone. 'Young man, if you don't stop playing games with God, you'll die a fiery death,' Reverend said. Butch walked out. Never stepped foot in a church after that, as far as I know."

Mom shook her head and lowered it. She locked her fingers together over her lap.

"That stayed with Butch," Mom said. "He went AWOL from the army; afraid he'd die in a blast. He'd freeze to death before he'd let a kerosene heater in that old trailer of his. Turned to the drink, but never to the Lord."

Miss Lorraine looked down at the floor.

I had just been listening to Uncle Walter in the back of the room. I never considered that what happened to Uncle Butch was more than an accident.

I brushed my hand over Mom's sleeve. It slid up. I noticed bruises. This was something I'd seen a few times before. Each time I saw it, it caused an ache in my gut, the feeling of wrong.

Mom was quick to pull her sleeve back down.

"What does it mean to play games with God?" I asked Mom.

"The Bible says to be cold or hot. If you are lukewarm, God will spit you out of his mouth. It means *you* choose good or bad. There's nothing between."

Her words confused me more. I never thought of Uncle Butch as bad. In fact, when he cuffed up my dad for hurting my mom, I found Butch to be downright good. My father stood behind a pulpit, but he put his hands on Mom. That was worse, I thought, than anything Uncle Butch had ever done.

The photo of the accident came back to my mind. Then what Ms. Lorraine said the reverend told Butch. A fiery death. It came true.

It was Reverend Hugill who gave a sermon at the funeral. He stood by Uncle Butch's urn. He was a big man with white hair in a black suit. When he spoke, his voice was so deep that I felt it in my chest. It silenced the room. The reverend gave us our due warning.

"We have a choice. God or Satan. Every man will die and stand before the Lord. Don't play games with God, lest you end up like Butch," Reverend said. "Do you know this day, beyond a shadow of a doubt, if you were to die, you'd make heaven your home?" he asked.

I shivered all over when he asked this. To the reverend's question, I thought, *I do not know.*

At the end of his sermon, folks went up to the reverend in tears.

He prayed for them as they stood with their heads low.

I wanted to go up too, but I was afraid. I couldn't move.

After the service, we all stepped outside the funeral home. I stood between my parents, regretting I hadn't gone to the reverend for prayer.

I heard the rumble of a jet and spotted its stream in the sky.

I grabbed Mom's hand and held it tightly. I swallowed hard, feeling my throat tight against my collar and my tie, too scared to slip it loose.

I imagined the jet would burst into flames overhead and crash down on us. It seemed if the reverend was right, that I played games with God. Same with my dad. Just like Butch, seemed a fiery death was fit for us all.

I imagined Great Uncle Walter would stand with a photo of the plane crash that killed us. He'd find my skull with his clouded magnifying glass. It would be there in the heap of the funeral home's wreckage, cratered into the ground with black smoke rolling from the crash.

AFTER THE HUNT

Travis came home late, high. He slipped in the back door and tried to walk past his mom in the kitchen. But she snatched him up by his hood.

"Let me see your eyes, stoner," she said.

Travis jerked away from her, but she didn't let loose.

"You're on the road to nowhere, just like your loser friends," Travis's stepdad Deak said as he came in the room.

"Coming from two drunks," Travis snapped.

"Who work and pay the bills," his mom said. She knocked Travis upside the head. Several times. Nicked him a good one with her long fingernails and drew a bit of blood. "You stay away from Aiden and Jay," Travis's mom said as she pushed him off.

So the night after, when Travis's mom and Deak left for the Rambler to drink and play darts, Travis was out the door to Aiden's house just a few minutes down the road.

There, Aiden called his older cousin several times to score some weed, but the dude blew him off. At least Jay, Aiden's other buddy, came through with a plastic liter of Baker's Club whiskey. The boys tipped it back and passed it around until car lights flashed through Aiden's front window, pulling into the driveway.

"Shit," Aiden said. "My mom."

The guys put on their jackets and hurried outside to the fire pit by Aiden's garage.

Jay passed the booze to Tyler, while Aiden got wood for a fire.

"Aren't you guys freezing?" Aiden's mom called up the yard, as she peeked her head through the sliding glass door of the house. It was, after all, November in Pennsylvania and probably in the mid-forties.

"No," the guys said.

Aiden sprinkled lighter fluid over the logs.

Travis yanked his hood up.

Jay shoved the booze bottle in his jacket.

"Whatever," Aiden's mom said, shaking her head beneath the light above the back deck. "Keep that fire low."

"Mom!" Aiden snapped.

Aiden's mom flicked off the light and slid the door shut.

Aiden got a good fire going.

"I can't wait to turn seventeen next month," Aiden said. He scraped what little weed he had from a baggie into his bong. He took a lighter from his jacket, put his lips on the bong, and gave it a light. He puffed smoke as he exhaled. "I don't need parent permission to drop out of school. My mom doesn't have a say. I can walk into the principal's office and tell them all to fuck off."

"Then what are you going to do with yourself?" Jay asked.

"Party," Aiden said. He leaned back in his chair and handed the bong to Jay. "I dunno. Get a job at McDonald's or some shitty place, for now."

"Fuck school. I ain't dropping out. I just ain't going," Jay said. He took a hit. "What about you?" he asked Travis as he passed him the bong.

Travis just squeaked into auto mechanics at tech. He actually liked it. Also, Travis had been nagging his stepdad Deak for his old Jeep Wrangler. Deak promised he'd get it running for Travis if he could pass everything in the first quarter. Travis was pulling Cs, though he wasn't sure how long he could keep it up.

"Probably drop out," Travis said. He took a hit of the spent bunk ash in the bong. "Get some chick pregnant. Live off my mom," he said, sounding all serious.

Aiden and Jay laughed.

Around eleven thirty that evening, Travis figured he'd push off.

"Big hunting trip with the stepdad tomorrow," he said as he put his hands on the arms of his lawn chair and hoisted himself up.

"Ah, that's right. Still haven't bagged a buck," Aiden jeered.

Jay laughed, that really irritating, asshole, stoner friend laugh.

"Fuck off," Travis said as he stood.

Sure, Aiden and Jay were nearly high school dropouts, but they'd both bagged their deer. Jay actually had three kills under his belt. Two bucks and a doe. Travis still hadn't made a kill. This bugged him to hell and back.

Aiden pretended to hold an invisible rifle at Travis. "Pow," he said, cocking the imaginary shaft and clicking his finger over an invisible trigger.

Jay laughed.

Travis turned and gave his friends a middle finger over the shoulder. He wished he could peel out of Tyler's driveway in that Wrangler. Instead, he walked the berm home.

Travis remembered the fuss Deak made when he was twelve, when he finished his hunter's safety course, leaned the rules of gunmanship, the biggest being *never point a gun at anyone*. Deak, a handsome brick-of-a-man with a Fu Manchu mustache, beamed ear-to-ear when the ranger pinned that hunting license on Travis's camouflage hat. Travis was a decent shot, and he saw something in Deak that was like, OK, now here's something Travis might actually be good at. Ever since then, Travis looked forward to hunting camp with the prospect he'd bag his buck. However, with all the arguing at home and the way he felt toward Deak of late, the trip to camp wasn't terribly appealing. Then again, though, buck season was near religion. And the Friday through Monday trip was one of the few excused absences Travis could guarantee this school year from Deak and his mom.

Travis got home around quarter till twelve, glad there was no sign of Deak or his mom home from the bar.

Travis passed through the living room, where Deak displayed all of his prized kills. There were two eight-point buck mounts on either side of the fireplace, a stuffed jake on the hearth, two pheasants on the mantle, and a black bear head in the center of the stone chimney. There was also a family photo of Travis as a first grader with Deak and his mom on the mantle. In the photo, Travis hung over Deak's shoulders. They were all smiles back then. Travis's mom looked young, her face round and full.

Travis flipped the photo off on the way to his room.

Travis never knew his real dad. Deak came along when Travis was five. Deak was all the *world's number one dad* stuff splayed over coffee mugs. It was a life of little league, motocross, hunting, and fishing. Too bad Travis always struck out, always finished last. Never bagged that buck. Travis spent the years watching Deak choke back his pride, still, while encouraging him. "We'll get 'em next time," Deak would say. Worse, Deak was the champion, it seemed, of everything. "Ah, Deak, man. What a good guy. He was always the best [fill in the blank]," folks would say when they realized Travis was Deak's stepson. Deak was a master mechanic. If it was broke, Deak could fix it. He was the kind of guy a football gravitated to like a magnet to metal. Meanwhile, Travis gave it his all, jutted back and forth trying to catch a pass. However, the football usually slipped through Travis's arms and bounced on the turf. Travis was lanky, awkward. A far cry from the bright-eyed, broad-shouldered, all-around charmer Deak. Travis noticed how women looked twice when Deak walked by. No surprise, Deak was always screwing around. Travis's mom drank on account of it.

Travis peeled off his clothes. He sprayed them with Febreze, hoping to mask the smell of the booze, bunk weed, and campfire. He slid into bed. He slipped his hand down the top of his underwear thinking about this strawberry blond girl Kaylie from school. He stopped though at the sound of Deak's new F-150 pulling into the drive.

Travis heard Deak and his mom barge through the front door. His mom said something about some whore and Deak said, "Ah, don't start!"

Travis stayed quiet in bed, wondering if they'd check in to be sure he was home.

He envisioned the dark stream of eyeliner from his mom's tears as he listened to her and Deak argue.

Maybe, if the man kept it in his pants, Travis thought.

When Deak and Travis's mom went rounds, she'd get violent and swing on Deak. She'd try to leave, but Deak would hide her keys. She'd ransack the house or throw back shots all hours of the night and be heard puking up her guts in the toilet at four A.M.

Some mornings, Travis would find Deak sleeping alone on the couch. Some, he'd find his mom passed out on the sofa in a snoring Deak's arms. Some, he'd find Deak or his mom had taken off, then one or the other would slip in the door all apologetic in a couple days or so.

That particular night, Travis heard the back door slam. Someone peeled out of the drive. It sounded like Travis's mom's car screeching onto the road. The way she sped off, he prayed to God she didn't get herself killed. He called her phone seven times in a row to check on her, give her an earful, but she didn't pick up once.

• • •

In the morning, Deak woke Travis for the three-hour trip north to camp in Tionesta, Pennsylvania. Travis was already packed. He hopped out of bed in a blur. He threw on some clothes and grabbed his satchel of hunting gear.

Travis and Deak hit the road.

Travis had a hangover. He slept most of the way to Tionesta but woke up on the dirt road leading up to camp through a cold November downpour. The F-150 cab rocked over potholes. The suspension creaked. The plush dice in the mirror swayed. Travis braced his elbow in the window frame and gripped the *oh-shit* handle above the passenger door as Deak steered around muddy tire ruts.

They reached a spot in the road, washed out with a deep puddle. Travis worried about the truck flipping as Deak ramped the hillside to skirt the puddle. Travis envisioned the truck crashing against trees over the bank. Instead, the tires spun through the muck. Deak steered against the fishtail with his broad hands and hairy knuckles tight on the steering wheel.

Travis steadied the hunting gear in the back of the cab from crashing against the passenger door. He caught Deak's wolf-blue eyes under his hunting cap in the rearview mirror.

"We would have spit right through in the old Wrangler," Deak said as he steered the truck back, flat onto the road.

There it was, the bait, bringing up the Wrangler. *Dangle the carrot*, Travis thought. Travis had to admit, he'd kill to get that thing on the road. If he kept his end of the bargain with his grades, Deak would get it running for sure.

"There was a twelve-point spotted at Hollis's crossing," Deak said.

"Cool," Travis said. He imagined shooting a deer with a rack like that. Not a spike. Not a four-point. Not a six. A twelve. That would more than make up for all that time Travis hadn't bagged a buck.

Travis looked out his window and caught his reflection in the side mirror. Travis noticed in his face every trace of a boy. He postured up in his seat and made his expression go stern. "Thunderstruck" by ACDC played on the radio. Travis cranked it up.

Deak skirted the potholes the rest of the way down the driveway to camp.

The low-slung cabin and the shed that matched its size hugged the strawy grassland.

Deak parked the truck beside the cabin.

Travis remembered when he was a kid, when Deak bought the acreage next to the marsh to build the cabin. Travis remembered loading up the stone for the fireplace with his mom and Deak, carrying it in his little arms.

Deak tossed Travis the keys.

Travis gathered his things from the truck. He walked onto the porch, unlatched the padlock, opened the door, and dropped his bag and gear on the floor.

He took in the musk of camp, an open room with a fireplace on one wall, a kitchenette, and a little bathroom on the other.

Travis walked across the flakeboard floor and dropped face-first into the brown twill sofa. That bit of booze at Aiden's, eating nothing earlier in the morning, then the bumpy road to camp made his headache worse. He needed more rest.

Deak came in and out, stacked firewood, and unpacked things from the cooler while Travis slept.

Travis woke early in the evening. He ate some Slim-Jims and pounded a Mt. Dew. He found Deak tinkering with the quads in the shed. Deak made some burgers from venison on a charcoal grill for dinner. Travis and Deak ate outside on the porch in spite of the damp chill. They shot in their guns just off the porch into the old targets tacked on trees across the marsh. On the first shot, Travis's twelve-gauge kicked when it fired and knocked his shoulder back. He was sure to steady it up when he fired. Deak got four bullseyes with his twenty-gage. Travis got near the bullseye twice, but never quite nailed it. It seemed the harder Travis tried, the worse he shot.

Deak offered Travis a Natty Ice beer.

Travis hesitated.

"What? You don't drink?" Deak asked.

Travis took the beer can. He shook his head, looked away, and popped the tab.

"Hair of the dog," Deak said. Then he took a big gulp of his beer.

They went to bed around eleven o'clock.

Before sunrise, Travis and Deak geared up in camo and set off on their quads for their tree stand.

They parked at the footpath leading to the stand, which overlooked a clearing in the woods.

On the path, Deak stopped to check some salt licks he'd put out during his last visit to the camp.

"Decent activity," Deak said.

"Hell yeah," Travis said looking at the wear on the licks.

When they reached the tree stand, Travis passed the hunting gear up the ladder to Deak. Everything Deak told Travis to do—"Hand me my gear, my gun," felt like an order. As Travis passed up the guns, Deak yelled out, "Careful." Deak's tone, like he was scolding some little kid, put Travis on edge.

Travis climbed onto the stand and sat quietly next to Deak.

They waited for deer.

It had been a few hours, and Deak and Travis hadn't spotted anything besides a squirrel. Travis grew bored, discouraged. Then it started to drizzle rain. The dampness caused a chill. Maybe this wouldn't be the year after all, Travis conceded. He knew hunting was all a waiting game. But he thought of all the hours he'd spent over the years, just waiting for nothing. It was enough for him to call it a day and head back to camp.

Deak looked out into the woods, his back to Travis. Travis sharpened his eye through the scope of his gun which was strapped over his shoulder. He eyed left from the white birch in the woods. His eye followed the scope to Deak's back. The scope magnified the camouflage of Deak's jacket in a hazy close-up. It was a terrible thought, an odd thought, broke *the* carnal role of gunmanship— But it would be easy to take Deak out.

Then, Travis heard cracking twigs in the distance. He turned his torso far right, back to the birch trees. He spotted a strapping buck facing him in his scope. He adjusted his position, kicked off the safety, and drew the sight lower. He turned the scope to sharpen his view a third of the way up the buck's chest. A double lung shot.

Travis heard Deak's voice, softly, felt his breath in his ear, "Get 'em, bud. He's yours."

Travis steadied his eye, braced his shoulder, and pulled his trigger.

The buck's hindquarter dropped. A stunned look flashed in its eyes. Its front legs buckled.

Travis let go of his gun, and it fell in the strap to his side. He scurried off the stand. As he put his foot on the ladder anchored in the tree trunk, Travis snagged his jacket on an old nail. He yanked his jacket back but lost his footing. He fell from the tree.

Deak jutted up from the stand, reaching out for Travis. But Travis was already in a free fall. The gun swung behind Travis. He landed hard, his back against the gun without his breath.

He rolled over onto his stomach, unable to stand, heaving in.

Deak rushed down the ladder after him.

Deak pulled Travis's upper body from the ground. He cradled Travis in his lap.

Travis looked up into Deak's eyes, still desperate for air.

"Breathe through it, buddy," Deak said.

Travis heaved, then finally breathed out.

"Knocked the wind out of you," Deak said. He put his hand firm on Travis's chest.

Deak helped Travis to his feet. He lifted the gun strap over Travis's head and sat it in the grass. Deak pulled Travis's camo jacket and shirt up to look over Travis's flesh.

"You scraped your ribs to hell and back," Deak said, lowering the shirt back down.

Travis moved his elbows, his knees. He felt over his body, to see if he'd broken anything.

"That's a hell of a fall," Deak said. "Twenty feet, at least." He picked up Travis's gun and looked it over.

"You want to wait here. I'll trail the buck," Deak said.

"I'll go. I want to," Travis said.

They headed toward the buck.

Travis pained, the more he moved. Mostly in his ribs at first. He struggled to keep up with Deak. He noticed he couldn't put much pressure on his right leg, around the ankle. Every time he tried to walk normally at the heel, a stabbing pain shot up his calf. He limped, putting pressure on the shoulder of his sole.

Travis and Deak reached the buck. Still in the grass where it was shot. It hadn't died yet. It trembled and made a horrible crying sound. It flailed its neck as though trying to get up, but its legs appeared paralyzed.

"Your kill. Finish 'em off," Deak said. He handed Travis his gun.

Travis looked at Deak, wide-eyed. *Why can't you do it?* he thought. But Travis dared not ask.

He took the rifle from Deak and aimed it at the buck's neck as the buck cried out. He pulled the trigger. Travis flinched at the sound of the gunshot and found his eyes had shut.

The buck's crying stopped.

Travis opened his eyes.

Deak crouched over the buck and counted its rack. "Twelve-points. Way to go, Trav," Deak said.

There was a pitch of excitement in Deak's voice, that something Travis seemed to have been waiting for all his life.

Travis leaned over the buck and counted the points for himself.

A sharp pain shot from Travis's ankle up through his shin. Travis put his hands on his knees and hoisted himself back up with a groan.

"Deak. I think I really messed up my ankle," Travis said. He lifted his pant leg. His leg was swollen from the knee down and throbbed.

"Can you still help with the buck?" Deak asked, looking over the distance to the quads. They looked like two tiny dots down the trail on the other side of the grassy marsh.

"Got to," Travis said. No way Deak could drag the big deer himself.

So, Travis and Deak dragged out the buck. They stopped a couple of times, so Travis could nurse his leg and breathe through the pain.

Travis nearly cried when he pushed the buck's carcass with his knee as he struggled to help Deak load it on the cart at the back of Deak's quad.

Travis trailed Deak on the quads back to camp. He watched the buck's neck sway over the potholes of the trail. Finally, Travis could tell Aiden and Jay, he bagged his buck. A twelve point, at that. *Good things are worth the wait,* Travis thought, trying to focus on his accomplishment, rather than the pain. He positioned his hurt foot on the peg of the quad to ease the impact of every bump, rut, and root on the path.

Back at camp, Deak and Travis unloaded the buck outside the shed in the brown grass. Deak kept asking Travis about his ankle.

"Maybe it's sprained. It'll be alright," Travis said.

Deak pulled his knife from his belt strap and handed it to Travis. "Pull up on the white hairs of the stomach pouch. Cut through the skin, blade-up," Deak said.

Travis lifted the skin and poked in the blade. As much as he'd imagined shooting a deer, that's where the idea of the kill had always ended. He'd never envisioned suffering, the need to shoot close range to put the buck down. He'd never gutted a deer, assumed it was something Deak would just do. Travis sliced into the buck's flesh. Its cry from the close-range shot, the desperate flash in its eyes came to mind. Travis's hand started to shake. He buckled at the knees and let go of the knife.

Deak cradled Travis from behind and guided him, hand-over-hand, to the knife. Travis's bloodied hands trembled, as Deak led his hand through the skin pouch to the tail, then back up through the sternum of the carcass.

They flayed the stomach open. Deak helped Travis yank out the windpipe of the buck. It felt odd, like a slimy rubber hose, and came loose with a snap, like the break of bone or cartilage. Then, Deak guided Travis's hands into the top of the innards. They scooped them out. The pink organs and intestines spilled onto the grass, leaving a blood-filled cavern in the deer's gut.

Travis fought his eyes from looking away into the marsh while he and Deak pulled the carcass into the shed where the deep-freeze buzzed, ready for storing the hunt. Deak strapped the buck up by the legs to a mount made for skinning that hung from the roof beam of the shed. They struggled, bore down all their weight at the elbows on the chain of the deer mount, to pull the deer up.

Travis had been with Deak when he bagged his last eight-point, but it was a clean kill. Travis kept reimagining the way his buck dropped, the flash in the eye, his own fall from the tree and the feeling of not being able to breathe. Messin' around with the gun at Deak's back. He felt sorry for that. This all kept running through his mind. He'd never before considered the sting of suffering, what it really meant, what it might be like.

He watched Deak skin the buck.

By the time dusk set in, Travis's leg throbbed. His adrenaline waned.

"I'm spent, Deak," he said. He leaned against the door.

"Imagine so," Deak said.

Travis's nerves had worsened. He fought tears. He jumped at the ripping sound as Deak's broad back yanked down the buckskin, revealing more of the buck's muscly flesh.

"Mind if I go inside?" Travis asked. He cupped his hand on his hurt leg.

Deak looked up.

Travis caught Deak, eye-to-eye.

"Go wash up. Maybe pack some ice, prop your leg up. Nothing like a cold beer after a kill. Best you ever had in your life," Deak said.

Travis nodded. He limped inside the camp.

He undressed in the bathroom. He limped into the shower. He pressed his head against the wall as the water fell over him. He felt as though he could wash down the drain with the blood of the buck.

After the shower, Travis dressed. He went into the kitchen and filled a bag with ice cubes for a compress. He limped to the sofa and hoisted his leg on the coffee table. He thought of getting that beer, that it might calm his nerves, but he decided he'd better not.

After an hour or so, Deak burst through the door. He held the buck's severed head up by the horns with his strong arms.

"This is a mount, buddy," Deak said. "We'll put him right in the center of the fireplace at the house."

Deak sounded like the *number one dad* from the picture on the mantle back home, playing up some big accomplishment to a five-year-old Travis.

"For sure," Travis said, locking in on Deak's proud, smiling face.

Deak went back out the door, back to the shed.

Night settled in. A cold front moved in. Frost settled over the marsh. From the cabin window, under the full white moon, the grass looked blue. The chilly wind gusts whistled through the gaps in the cabin walls and the room was a chill.

Travis thought of Deak butchering the buck out in the cold. He put on a kettle for warm coffee for Deak. He lined the fireplace with paper and wood and gave it a light. He felt it was the least he could do after all Deak had done. Not just the gutting, the skinning—a sum of everything over the years.

Deak's tired face seemed to soften when he came into the cabin to settle in for the night and set eyes on the fire in the hearth.

• • •

The worst of the three weeks following the hunt had nothing to do with Travis's broken ankle, the clumsy boot, and crutches.

Travis's mom and Deak had a big fight, again over *the whore*, and Deak left the house. Travis genuinely expected things would blow over like they always did between Deak and his mom. He was sure Deak would strut in the door any day with flowers, and they'd make up again. But three days passed. Then, four. A week went by, and there was no sign of Deak. Travis got to thinking *the whore* had to be more than a hook-up. She had to be someone Deak thought a lot of. Maybe even loved.

Travis told Aiden and Jay how he lined the twelve-point up in his scope. Travis showed off his cast. "Doesn't hurt all that bad," he said, moving his leg about. He let on that the buck died in one shot. He left out everything that happened after the fall. He left out that Deak split shortly after the hunt. Instead, Travis talked up how Deak planned to move his bear mount and put Travis's twelve-point in the center of the stone fireplace back home once the taxidermy was done.

"Did you gut your deer, skin 'em?" Travis asked Aiden.

"No," Aiden said. "We paid a guy to do it."

"My uncle always does that," Jay said.

"Deak and I did ours," Travis said, feeling proud.

But Aiden didn't ask anything about it. Instead, he called his weed-dealer cousin. "Asshole," Aiden said, as his cousin's cell rang through to voicemail. Then he yacked about how horrible a place McDonalds was to work. "You should have seen the bitch Nazi manager's face there when

I told her to fuck off. I threw my apron on the counter and walked the fuck out," Aiden said.

"You only lasted two weeks," Jay said.

"Too weeks, too long. You have any idea how bad that place smells?" Aiden asked.

Travis raised his brow, bit his lip. "Well," he said. "Better push off. School tomorrow."

"Oh yeah, forgot you're still a Rhodes scholar," Aiden said.

Aiden and Jay laughed.

Travis shrugged them off.

Travis walked home with the ache of his leg in the boot and his breath visible in the cold.

When Travis got home, he found his mom on the sofa, crying. He figured she was drunk.

"It's really over for good this time," she said, but there was no slur of her words. She raised her arm out to Travis with a desperate look on her face.

Travis sat beside her on the sofa. He sniffed, but he didn't smell any booze.

His mom put her head on his shoulder and wept. Travis's instinct was to jerk away from her, but he stayed put, even put his arm around her.

"Deak will come back. He always does," Travis said, just to put his mom out of her misery, even though he didn't believe his own words.

He looked past the boot on his foot, propped on the coffee table, over the hunting game mounts on the fireplace. He envisioned his buck back from taxidermy, given pride-of-place in the center of the hearth, just like Deak had promised. He recalled the look of the deer at the close-range shot, the skinning and gutting. Travis thought back on messing around with the gun at Deak's back on the hunt. Seemed now, Deak was out of his life. He knew he didn't mean anything by it, but in some strange way, he felt almost at fault that Deak was gone.

Travis looked down over his mom's head. He took in the coconut shampoo smell, felt the soft wisps of her dark hair tickle against his cheek. God, Travis hated the sound of his mom crying. It was all he could do to peck her head with a kiss.

After they sat a while, Travis's mom's cell phone rang. "Deak," she mouthed and jumped up in her seat.

Travis slipped off the sofa and into the kitchen while his mom talked to Deak. He didn't want to hear Deak's voice on the line, couldn't even stand to be in the house around it, so he threw on his jacket and slipped outside for air. Out in the cold, unsure of what to do, he decided to tinker with the old Wrangler in the driveway.

Travis popped the hood, looked over the hoses, wires, and parts. He took in the smell of oil, grease, and gas. He got a ratchet set from the garage. The alternator was where he figured he'd start stripping back the parts. He found the right size bit and cranked the ratchet to loosen the bolt mounting it near the motor. He scuffed and bloodied his knuckles when his hand slipped, prying at the stubborn bolt. Travis ignored the blood that surfaced at the top of the gashes on his knuckles. He leaned hard into the Wrangler to ease the weight off his foot. Travis mapped out the parts, undeterred by the numbness that set in his fingers from the cold.

Travis's mom peeked her head out the door with her phone in her ear. "The buck mount's done. Deak wants to know when to bring it by."

Travis didn't respond. He didn't acknowledge his mom.

"I guess Trav can't talk now," he heard his mom say. "So, you're look-ing for an apartment . . . If that's what you really want, what can I say?" Then, she slipped back inside the house and closed the door.

It was getting dark. Travis could barely see, but he couldn't stop loos-ening bolts and wires, prying on the alternator. It rocked a bit but was still fastened somewhere underneath.

Suddenly, the garage light shined into the drive. The door grinded open behind Travis.

Travis looked back.

His mom stood behind him and held a droplight. She plugged the cord in an outlet and turned it on. She pulled the light's long cord to Travis and hung it under the hood of the Wrangler.

"Shed a little light on the matter," she said.

Travis laid eyes on his mom, as she wiped the stream of eyeliner from beneath her eyes. She looked soft in the light. The fullness had returned to her face in her sober state.

"Why wouldn't you talk to Deak?" She asked. "He asked about you."

Travis shrugged. He fixed his eyes back on the motor.

The worst parts of the hunt flashed through his mind.

"Aren't you anxious for your buck mount?" she asked. "It's something to be proud of."

"I don't want it," Travis said.

His mom moved close behind him and moved her hand over the front of the Wrangler.

"Why not?" she asked.

Travis hesitated for a moment. "I pointed a gun at Deak's back when we were at camp," Travis said.

"Well, you didn't hurt him?" she asked.

"No," Travis said.

"Did he know?"

"No," Travis said.

"Well that was dumb," his mom said. She pulled at a loose wire on the alternator. "We all do things we regret."

Travis looked up at her. When he locked eyes with his mom, he could see in them the same pain as the dying buck.

"I'm sorry," she said. She softly put down the wire. She wrapped her hands over her forearms. "Freezing," she said and turned for the house. "*You* have to be the one to tell Deak you don't want the mount," she said with her back to Travis.

The idea of telling Deak that—just seeing him—gave Travis pause. He remained silent. He turned his attention back to the alternator, as his mom disappeared into the house. Behind him, he heard his mom go into the garage again, the sound of her car door, the turn of her engine.

"Where you headed?" Travis asked as she backed around him in the drive.

"Trav," she said. "I just got to get out a bit."

"You mean get drunk," Travis said, though he wasn't sure his mom had even heard him.

She backed out onto the road and sped off.

Travis turned back to the Wrangler, longing to speed off, just like that. Just like Deak. Just like his mom. Come hell or high water, he thought, sure as he bagged that buck, that Wrangler would run.

UNDER THE TABLE

Who cares if they ran me out of the fort in the woods? None of those boys own *Dukes of Hazzard*. Especially not Danny Drasky. Who says a boy can't play Daisy Duke?

Well, Danny doesn't know I stole his Matchbox General Lee on my way out of the fort.

I head down the path from the woods to my house. I can feel the little General Lee against my leg in my pocket. I imagine the look on Danny's face when he realizes it's gone. He might think he lost it, have all the boys search for it. He might figure I stole it, but by then, he'll be too late to catch me.

The path from the woods comes out between my yard and our neighbor's, old Ms. Cunningham's. I step through her grass. I rip a fistful of the pink peony blossoms that grow next to her house, since they happen to be near me. I toss them in front of me, like real hard, but the pedals just float gently as I move along. Some stick to my shirt.

My mom appears from the corner of our house on her way to Ms. Cunningham's back door.

"Mom," I call out, as I run toward her.

I want to tell her what happened in the woods—well, the part about being run off. Not about the car. I reach her and throw my arms around her waist.

"Danny Dra—" is all I get out.

"Quit your whining," Mom says. She pulls my head against her hip.

Ms. Cunningham comes to her back door. "Hello," she says.

Mom brushes my bangs from my forehead with her hand.

We step up onto the porch.

"Shoo," Mom says to the cats on Mrs. Cunningham's porch. The cats eat milk and bread from the old pie tins Ms. Cunningham puts out. A white, a tabby, and a tiger cat all scurry off.

"Oh, the cats are no bother," Ms. Cunningham says. Then, she waves us into the house with her arm.

In the doorway, Ms. Cunningham stoops over to kiss me on the cheek. Her lips are red and wet. She peers over the top of her glasses at me. She grabs my chin. Then, she gets her handkerchief from her shirt pocket and dries my eyes and nose.

"Did I see you out the window ripping up my posies?" Ms. Cunningham asks. "It's a sad world for a boy who destroys pretty things. Now what's the fuss?"

"There's always a fuss with that one," Mom says.

"Why don't you go get Dolly," Ms. Cunningham says. "Only if you can be ginger with her. She's upstairs on the footstool in my room."

Dolly is an old Barbie that Ms. Cunningham and Mom let me play with. Only when I'm at Ms. Cunningham's place though.

"Promise," I say, looking deep into Ms. Cunningham's kind eyes.

Then, I dash up the steps to fetch Dolly.

I pick Dolly up from the footstool upstairs. I move my finger across her pretty face. She's old. Mom says from the fifties. She has curly red bangs, big blue eyes, and a black and white swimsuit. I pull the General Lee from my pocket to show Dolly. I run the little car over the foot stool at her feet. Then I take Dolly and the General with me downstairs. I peek around the landing at the bottom of the stairs. My mom and Ms. Cunningham's backs are turned at the sink talking. I think it is a fun idea to spy on them a bit, and I slip under the table. Surely, they don't know I'm there. The lace tablecloth hangs over the sides of the table, like a roof to my very own fort. *Who needs one in the woods with the other boys?*

"You and your cats. Psst. Down now, Suzie Thomas! Nothing like a cat's arse in your face while you're sipping tea," Mom says.

The kettle on the stove hisses softly.

"Don't you mind old Suzie Thomas," I hear Ms. Cunningham say.

With a soft thud, Suzie Thomas appears like magic on all fours near the edge of the table. A fine, fat, old tiger cat with a pink collar, Suzie Thomas stays low to the floor. The cat comes under the table and rubs against me. Then it slips around the leg of the table, out of sight at the stairs.

"And what a name for a cat, at that," Mom says.

I hear a noise at the screen door. I peek under the tablecloth. I see two pairs of legs sticking out of two pleated, khaki skirts. Brown nylons. White loafers. One's ankles are thick and fat, like dough. The others are thin and nice. Not like they belong to a plump lady, though they do.

It's old Mrs. Goss, Ms. Cunningham's sister, and Mrs. Goss's daughter, Mary Catherine.

"You'd have to have the good sense to know a girl cat from a boy cat," Mrs. Goss says, as the screen door creaks open. "How long did it take you, sister, five years to figure it out?" she asks.

"Oh balderdash," Ms. Cunningham says.

I lift the tablecloth to get a better look at the women.

Ms. Cunningham steps over to Mrs. Goss. She takes a covered dish and pecks her old sister on the cheek. She comes toward the table, so I slide back to the middle of it to keep my cover. She sits the dish on the table. It clanks above me.

"Maybe six," Ms. Cunningham says, laughing. "Hey, I don't go 'round inspecting cat genitals with a magnifying glass. I'll never forget the vet's face when he told me *she* was a *he*. So, I just added the *Thomas* for good measure. Whatever *it* was, I reckoned, *it* was up to Suzie Thomas to decide."

The women all laugh.

"Where's the boy?" Mary Catherine asks.

Even under the table, I can smell Mary Catherine's dank, old perfume and the hairspray on her perfect blue hair. Mom says Mary Catherine looks awfully old for her sixties. I envision her face, which is round and wrinkly and always full with a smile.

"Up playing with that old doll again," my mom says.

I pull the doll close to my chest.

"Aren't you afraid that boy will turn queer?" Mary Catherine asks.

"Better queer than like the rest," my mom says.

I think on the word queer—I hear it means strange.

The women laugh again.

"Isn't that the truth," Ms. Cunningham says.

"Oh, there's no harm in a boy playing with a doll," Mrs. Goss says.

"As long as he only plays with it here," my mom says. She raises her voice, I think, so I can hear upstairs, where she thinks I still am. "His dad would stomp him into the lawn if he found out."

"Let the boy be," Ms. Cunningham says. "Besides, I heard you caterwauling on the porch last night, after your husband's car tore up the road. He's stomped you into the ground a time or two."

The room gets quiet.

"He's running around again," I hear my mom say. "I wouldn't care so much, but he spends all the money on the whore."

"Who is it this time?" Mary Catherine asks.

"Angie Davis," my mom says.

I put my hand over my mouth. I've heard mom use the word *whore* when she gets angry about the women who run around with my dad. Because of this, I know it's bad. I imagine Angie Davis. She's the lady, I'm pretty sure, that works at the little post office down the road. Bright red hair. Great big boobs. Shirts so tight they look like skin. A little like Dolly but with wonky teeth, I think, looking down at the Barbie.

"That old cat! She'd lie with anything," Mrs. Goss says.

"Men!" Ms. Cunningham says. "The only man I had ran off with my sister. I haven't had one cross my door stoop since."

I imagine Ms. Cunningham, how she stands firm at her front door every time my dad comes over. What she says is true.

"Hey," Mrs. Goss says. "Lucky you. I had to put up with him for thirty years."

"And how long did it take you to figure out *he* was queer?" Ms. Cunningham asks.

The women laugh.

"That's my father you're talking about," Mary Catherine says.

"Well, I'd say in our first year of marriage. I came home and found him in my chiffon. God rest his soul," Mrs. Goss says.

"Dear God, Mother," Mary Catherine says.

"What can I say? The girl's proof. I tried my best," Mrs. Goss says through a snort.

The women laugh even louder.

I can't help but laugh with them this time. I put my hand over my mouth again, so I don't blow my cover. My mom has a pink dress she calls chiffon. It looks like a peony. I imagine an old, bald man twirling about in it. I think Mr. Goss has been dead for a long time. I never knew him. I imagine he might look like Boss Hog from *The Dukes*. What does it hurt? I think. Girls wear pants. Why can't men wear chiffon?

The women carry on laughing and talking and milling about the kitchen. I hear the clank of china being set out on the table; the stir of a kettle coming to a soft whistle on the old cook stove; the sound of drawers opening and closing with silverware. I hear the sound of the cookie tin being pried open.

I try to keep quiet, but I can't stop thinking of Boss Hog in a chiffon. My laughter bursts from under the table and gives me away.

"What on earth?" I hear Mary Catherine say.

Mary Catherine's face appears beneath the tablecloth. As she stoops, her rosy, chubby cheeks droop around her round, little nose.

"Why you rascal," she says.

"Under the table, of all places," Ms. Cunningham says.

"God help those little ears," I hear Mrs. Goss say.

"For Christ's sake," Mom says.

"This is my fort. I'm not moving," I say.

Mary Catherine says, "I think any other boy might try and peek up the skirt, but—"

"I think we'll be alright," I hear Ms. Cunningham say.

The women laugh again, including my mom. Who'd peek up a skirt? I wonder. I've already seen Ms. Cunningham's plain, white bloomers on the line. I can't imagine Mrs. Goss's or Mary Catherine's would look any different. Now, Daisy Duke, curling her long, spider legs in the window of the General Lee . . . That's a different story. Heck, you couldn't cram a bloomer under those jean shorts of Daisy's, I reckon. That's why I pretended to kick off imaginary bad guys on my tiptoes back at the fort, like

Daisy does in heels. I tied my T-shirt in a knot above my belly button, just like Daisy does. Well, until Danny Drasky said, "Disgusting. Man, you a sicko or something? Really, a boy acting like a girl." Then, all the other boys said, "Ew."

The smell of butter crisps from the tin fills the air. Ms. Cunningham hands me one under the table. I snatch it out of her hand and take a bite. The cookie melts in my mouth and crumbles down my shirt.

I hear the women pour out the tea kettle into cups on the table.

Then, there's a knock at the screen door.

"Hello," Ms. Cunningham says.

"Is Jimmy there?" I hear a boy ask.

I know that voice. It's Danny Drasky. I peer under the tablecloth. I see his legs through the screen door. The other boys, too, stand with him on the porch. They have sticks, and they clank them against the floor.

"Is Jimmy here?" Ms. Cunningham calls out in the room like a mockingbird.

"We want him to come play with us," Danny says.

I slide to the back of the table, away from the door, so the boys can't see me. I hold Dolly firm. I hide the General Lee under my leg. I do not answer, thinking I've got the best of both worlds, a girl toy and a boy toy and no one to bother me.

"I guess he's not here," Ms. Cunningham says.

"You boys best be running along now," Mary Catherine says.

I smile.

The boys scatter off the porch.

Suzie Thomas leaps from the landing of the stairs onto the table. Something gets knocked over and clinks above my head.

"Shoo," Mom says, and she stomps by the table.

Suzie Thomas thuds back down on the floor. The old cat lands firm on its feet.

The women settle into their chairs for tea. Their legs come together under the table and wall in my fort.

LISA FRANK COSMOS

Evie Krauss looked out of the bus window that sunny Monday morning. She counted every sign in every yard about the stupid benefit spaghetti dinner for Maggie Smeal's daddy. There were five. They all read, HELP COACH SMEAL. Evie wondered why they hadn't taken them down. The dinner was over on Saturday, and Evie longed for one less daily reminder of what happened. Yes, Evie's ma was on drugs when she crashed into Maggie Smeal's daddy and hurt him. Bad. It was all everyone in town talked about. Let's get on with life, Evie thought. It had been three months since the accident. But still, the other kids on the bus turned their heads away just at the sight of Evie, like *she* was the one who'd done something wrong. Only Bruce from Evie's class had the balls to ask about her ma. "She's really like my older sister. We weren't close. I was raised by my grandma, Meme," Evie told Bruce. And all that was true.

The bus pulled up to the school just as Maggie got dropped off by her dad in his shiny, new, red Mustang. Maggie got out of the car in a new paint-splash, denim jumper dress with lace leggings and a new Lisa Frank backpack. Maggie's dad waved her off from the driver seat of their car. There was talk of pins and rods in the man's bones, but Evie couldn't help but notice he still drove just fine.

Evie looked down at her old jeans. They were threadbare at the knees. They had marker scribbles all over them from the last time Evie was bored in class. She tugged at the dragon logo on her yard sale polo. Then, she yanked the small fitting shirt down to her waistband. This was the first time she'd given her wardrobe, all the things she grabbed folded from the laundry basket, a thought.

In homeroom, Maggie showed off her new super deluxe Lisa Frank art kit with coloring pages, stickers, and markers to Tracy McBride. Before the accident, Evie and Maggie were close friends, but Maggie hadn't talked to Evie since. Then, Tracy horned in.

Evie stood on her tiptoes to get a good look at the kit.

Evie had asked for the Lisa Frank set just this past weekend, but Meme looked it over at K-Mart and said that it cost too much. Meme said Evie could get just-as-nice coloring books and stickers at the Dollar Store instead. Evie moved towards Maggie and Tracey to see the kit up close. She got near enough to the back of them to smell the fabric softener of their clothes. But Tracy looked back sharply at Evie with a scowl. She put her arm around Maggie and blocked Evie out.

Mrs. Morgan, whose desk was just a few feet away from Maggie's at the front of the class, looked up from marking papers.

"Evie Krauss," she said. "Leave Maggie alone."

Evie folded her arms, walked to her desk in the back of the room, and quietly cried.

Later, during recess, Evie asked to go inside to the bathroom. Instead, she went into the empty, third-grade classroom. She opened the top of Maggie Smeal's desk and set her eyes on the super deluxe Lisa Frank activity set. It didn't even have a finger smudge on the glossy cover. The big pegasus with rainbow wings on the kit looked alive. Evie imagined it would bat its big, long lashes, come to life, and carry her to other worlds. Unfortunately, it was Maggie's pegasus, though. The thought of Maggie on that horse! It made Evie's eyes tear again. Then, thoughts of the benefit dinner signs and Mrs. Morgan's scolding that morning washed over her.

Evie reached for a black Sharpie from the cup holder on Mrs. Morgan's desk. She scribbled over every cute, big-eyed, pink leopard and every purple wolf floating in the starry Lisa Frank universe. And that big pegasus? Evie x-ed out its eyes. Then, she rifled through the rest of the case. She tore every coloring page (the really nice ones with the black, velvety stuff outlining every form). She shredded every brightly colored sticker sheet. She crumbled them in her fists and scattered them like snowflakes into Maggie's desk. She dropped the top of the desk and ran back outside.

When the class returned from recess, Mrs. Morgan started the physical science lesson.

"Before you get out your workbooks, without looking . . ." Mrs. Morgan said, "Does anyone remember the definition of the cosmos?"

When no one raised their hand to answer, Mrs. Morgan put her fists on her hips. Her eyes widened at the quiet class.

"No one?" she asked. "Was no one listening to yesterday's lesson? Perfect order. Remember. Though the universe looks like chaos—remember that word—the ancient Greeks believed that the stars, and the planets, and the galaxies are there by no accident. They are ordered in perfect harmony."

Then, Mrs. Morgan told the class to get out their science workbooks with the picture of the earth on the cover.

Evie watched Maggie from the back of the class. Maggie's blond pigtails were tied with yellow yarn ribbon and hung long down her back. When Maggie opened her desktop, she stopped mid-lift. Her shoulders quivered. Then, she dropped the desktop and cradled her head in her arms.

Mrs. Morgan stopped the lesson. She leaned over Maggie and pulled at her arm. "What's wrong?" Mrs. Morgan asked.

Maggie lifted her head and opened her desk.

Evie would never forget the look on Mrs. Morgan's face. Mrs. Morgan's mouth fell open. Her cheeks grew flushed. She placed her hand in the center of her chest.

"Evie Krauss. Ms. Oletta's office. Now!" Mrs. Morgan said.

The other kids reared-up in their seats to see Maggie's desk, and they all let out a gasp. This was followed by the *trouble aww* of the class when someone was sent to the principal's office.

Evie walked down the aisle from her seat with her eyes to the floor. She suddenly felt awful for what she had done. Just the way the other kids looked at her put her near tears. *What on earth was she thinking?* Evie thought to herself.

Mrs. Morgan stashed the stuff back in the Lisa Frank case and stood with it at the front of the class. She handed it to Evie. The torn edges of the coloring sheets and the sticker pages stuck out of the edges, like something coming from a wound. Evie took the case in her arms. She walked slowly with it up to her elbows, careful not to spill anything out as she walked. She imagined the shame of picking the things up from the floor while her classmates looked on.

The school principal's office was just down the hall. When Evie arrived there, the secretary was on the phone with Mrs. Morgan, who called from the classroom when a student was in *that* big of trouble. The secretary was a fat woman with done-up red cheeks and gray, poofy hair. She was taking notes. Her pen stalled on the page, and she looked up at Evie with big eyes.

Evie sat in the waiting area near the secretary's desk, the Lisa Frank case flat in her arms. It felt like the time she found her old cat Snuffy dead next to the porch. He was stiff and odd, once the life had gone out of him. Evie recalled how she got Meme to come look at the cat. Meme fetched an empty shoebox for Snuffy's burial. Meme said, "Honey, these things just happen." Meme said the same thing about the car accident.

Ms. Oletta's office door was closed. The secretary knocked softly on it and said, "Sorry to disturb you." Evie caught a glimpse of Ms. Oletta, a tall, tan woman with can-curler hair. Ms. Oletta put the phone to her chest and raised her finger in the air. The secretary handed her the note and backed out the door.

Evie imagined Ms. Oletta would say, *After everything that's happened between you and Maggie, why would you do such a thing?*

Evie thought about her response. She figured she'd tell Ms. Oletta about the spaghetti dinner signs still all over town. She'd tell her about Maggie's daddy's new car, about Maggie's new clothes. She'd tell Ms. Oletta how badly she wanted a Lisa Frank set. *So, certainly, you must understand,* Evie imagined saying. *Oh, that is a lot,* she imagined Ms. Oletta would reply.

None of that was even the worst outcome of the accident though. Every fourth Saturday of every month since the car wreck, Evie and Meme would drive to the Galleria Mall. However, Evie never got to go inside. Instead, she and Meme would catch the Greyhound in the parking lot to visit her ma at the prison in some place called Munsy, Pennsylvania. This was a two-hour bus ride. Once they got to the visitor's center at the prison, Evie, Meme, and her ma sat awkwardly together on hard benches in a gray cafeteria. They were all desperate to come up with things to say to one another. Meme would break the silence by asking about the prison food. Then Evie's ma would talk about what she ate that week. She'd explain the food as either awful or not that bad. "Oh, eggbeaters," Meme would say with her nose scrunched up. Then Meme would put quarters in the vending machine to get them all Combos and Reese's Cups. "A little stale," Meme would say, taking a bite with the orange Reese's package in her hand. "Oh, I'm not complaining," Evie's ma would say. Meme would ask Evie, "How about yours?" "Little stale," Evie would say and shrug her shoulders. The hour-long visit was super awkward for Evie, who just thought at the sight of her ma, *What on earth have you done, woman, gone and ruined the perfectly good Saturday off from school?* Then, there was the goodbye hug. Evie would stiffen up with her arms tight to her sides when her ma put her arms around her. Evie had to turn her head when her ma kissed her cheeks. She could feel her ma's tears against her skin. To boot, after all that, it was another two-hour ride on the dark bus back home. At night. With nothing to do. Evie turned in her seat and watched the teenage girl behind her with the light of a handheld Nintendo shining in her face. The girl completely ignored her. Meme said, "Would it kill you to sit on your arse, Evie? Take a sleep, why don't you?"

This particular Saturday, when Evie and Meme got back to the house, Meme flicked on the TV. Maggie's daddy was on the late news . . . again. He stood with his arms in those weird crutches of his. The bottom of the screen read: *Community Comes Together for Former High School Football Hero and Beloved Coach Injured in Crash.* Seemed every time Maggie's dad was on the news, the bit ended with how Maggie's daddy was the quarterback who won state championships in '84. Then they'd say Evie's ma, the meth-addicted driver who crashed into his car, was now serving five years. Evie figured she'd tell Ms. Oletta how this made Meme cry. She'd tell her Meme stood in front of the TV and said, "My daughter is a person too. People make mistakes." Then, Meme said if she had the money, she'd get out of this god-forsaken, podunk town. Evie agreed with Meme and said it with her, "Yeah, my mom's a person too." She sneered at Maggie's daddy on the screen and folded her arms while he said how much he thanked the great people of this fine, little community for helping him through this terrible time. Then, at the end of the news clip, there was a shot of Maggie giving her daddy a hug. And when Evie said it wasn't fair, that she ought to—

Meme said, "Just keep hella' far from that Maggie Smeal girl."

Another thing Evie thought she might mention to Ms. Oletta was that Mrs. Morgan redid the seating chart in class. She put Evie and Maggie on the far, opposite corners of the room. Maggie, in the front. Evie, way in the back. Evie noticed the way Mrs. Morgan looked at Maggie, like poor, pretty, little Maggie. Oh, and after Mrs. Morgan scolded Evie to stay away from Maggie, Evie heard her tell Maggie how much she enjoyed the benefit spaghetti dinner. She said it was nice to see her daddy getting along after all he'd been through. This made Evie feel like she was nothing more than Maggie's daddy's near-killer's daughter.

After all that time waiting and thinking what she would say, Ms. Oletta called Evie into her office. Just as expected, Ms. Oletta looked up from the secretary's note and asked how Evie could do such a thing. Evie wanted to scream that Ms. Oletta, like everyone else in this god-forsaken town, already knew. However, Evie could not quite find the words. In fact, she just stood there, didn't have the good sense to take the seat at Ms. Oletta's desk. Instead, Evie put her head down. She cried into the ruins of the Lisa Frank cosmos and said, "I do not know."

• • •

Ms. Oletta had the secretary walk Evie outside to wait for Meme to pick her up. Evie overheard Meme on the phone tell Ms. Oletta she wasn't about to set foot in that school, not what with what she expected all those teacher friends of Coach Smeal thought of her.

Meme pulled up in her rust-red Buick. A cloud of blue smoke rolled from the muffler. Meme's big old car looked like a monster, and Meme sat at the driver's seat like some raging queen on her throne.

Evie didn't say a word when she settled onto the crazed pleather seat with the marred Lisa Frank case by her side. Neither did Meme.

Meme drove straight to K-Mart off of Route 80. She parked and got out of the car. Evie guessed she should follow, so she did. She could barely keep pace with Meme through the automatic doors, straight back to the kid's stationery aisle. Meme had misty eyes and her fists were all balled-up, like if she weren't in public, she'd whop Evie upside the head.

"It's this one, right?" Meme asked. "Who has the nine ninety-nine to waste, I'd like to know? What's in there, gold?"

Evie walked down the aisle toward Meme, half scared to say a word. She nodded yes at the sight of the pristine Lisa Frank deluxe art case. All its creatures were perfectly intact, smiling from their cosmos, just as they were before Evie had set her hands on Maggie's desk. Evie sobbed. One of those jags that grew heavier in her chest the more she tried to stifle it.

Meme riffled through her purse. She yanked out a wad of cash and took the Lisa Frank case from the clip on the shelf. She handed the kit and the money to Evie. Then, Meme hightailed it out of the aisle. Evie stood, wondering what to do. She thought maybe Meme headed to the ladies' clothes. She'd come back and walk Evie to the check-out. But when Evie stepped from the aisle, she saw Meme storm past Customer Service and out the door.

Evie headed to the register alone.

"You're awfully sad, for getting such a nice thing," the cashier said to Evie.

Evie worked at her composure, but she was too upset for words. She just nodded.

"Can't be that bad," the cashier said. She handed Evie the Lisa Frank case in a plastic K-mart bag and a handful of change.

The cashier had a cool, punk-rock look, like one of Lisa Frank's critters come to life. She had a rainbow-colored Mohawk that hung long, swept to the side. She had purple, thick-rimmed glasses with little jeweled stars in the corners. Her eyeshadow was bright blue. Her cheeks were pink. Her lips were bright red. Her jean jacket with cut-off sleeves and cool, sewn-on patches stuck out of her K-Mart smock.

Sure, Evie thought, as she left the store, that's what Lisa Frank would do. Send a spy, who was cool-looking and really nice, to make her feel really, super-duper, double-deluxe bad.

It was a quiet car ride home. When Meme parked in the driveway at the trailer, she said "I asked you one thing, to stay away from Maggie." Meme shook her head.

"I'm sorry," Evie said. "I know."

"You want to end up like your ma?" Meme asked. "Hell, what your mother caused was an accident. What you did, Evie, was downright cruel."

Meme got out of the car and slammed the door. Evie never felt so alone. The word accident made Evie think of what Mrs. Morgan said about the cosmos. Everything happened in perfect order. Evie would never say it to Meme, not any time soon, but if that were true, there were no accidents. Like the stars in the galaxy, that car wreck was already set perfectly in time.

That night, Evie sat through a stone-cold supper of SpaghettiOs. Meme acted like Evie wasn't even in the room. Meme looked through her glasses at her crossword puzzle on the table. She took the occasional bite of her Os.

After supper, Evie went straight to her room. She laid in her bed, staring up at the ceiling, until night fell outside her window. Through her sheers, she could see a few stars, sprinkled through the navy sky. She couldn't shake the thought of the vast cosmos.

Evie heard the creak of the door.

Meme peeked her head in the room.

"You up?" Meme asked.

Evie thought of pretending she was asleep, but she really wanted the *smooth-it-over* after the *good-talking-to* in the car.

"Yes," Evie said.

Meme's figure moved toward the bed.

"You had a rough one. We both did. It's just a tough time. For Maggie, too," Meme said. Just the mention of Maggie's name. Evie thought, *Why'd you have to bring her up?*

Then, Meme said, "None of us can change what happened. We just need to move on."

"I know," Evie said, thinking really, it was all the talk she expected from Meme. If anything, it was worth hearing for the touch of Meme's warm hand on her forehead.

Meme brushed away Evie's bangs.

"You can take two month's allowance for the kit," Evie said.

"Oh, I will," Meme said.

"I was thinking, Meme. You mind if I don't go to the prison next month?" Evie asked. "I don't like it there."

"You really think it's that bad?" Meme asked. "I was thinking we'd try the Lance peanut butter crackers in the vending machine next month. Well, maybe we should leave 'em for aliens to find after the end of the world . . . Maybe, I'll consider it, if you draw your ma a picture. You know, so we have something to talk about . . . besides lousy food. Now, get to sleep," Meme said.

Then Meme went out.

Evie had one of those nights where her thoughts drifted to dreams. She dreamed her ma wrecked a speeding meteor into a planet of Lisa Frank creatures, the brightly colored pegasus, leopards, and wolves. They were strewn through the cosmos, all maimed in the aftermath. Evie went about picking them up in her arms and nursing them. However, the more she frantically picked up, the more she found. Her arms became so full she couldn't hold onto them anymore.

Evie awoke sweaty and anxious. It took her a moment to realize it was all just a bad dream. She looked through the sheers at the stars in the endless, navy sky outside her window until she fell back asleep.

That Tuesday morning, Evie picked out a nice tie-dyed T-shirt. She paired it with black leggings and a bright pink, ruffled skirt. She got on the school bus with the new Lisa Frank folder in her lap. Evie counted only three spaghetti dinner signs still left out in yards.

The more Evie looked over the Lisa Frank folder, the more she thought it absurd. There was no such thing as a pegasus with rainbow wings. Purple foxes and multi-colored leopards weren't real. Then, there was what she'd learned in physical science. Space was black. Not pink, purple, and green. There were no Lisa Frank rainbows passing by like meteors. Furthermore, Lisa Frank creatures would need spacesuits to survive. There was little oxygen in the universe, after all.

Evie decided she'd make the best of things. She'd walk into homeroom and hand Maggie the Lisa Frank kit. She'd apologize. She wondered, when she did, if Maggie would even speak to her.

Yet at school, before the bell rang, while most of the students were still in the hall, Evie walked into class with the Lisa Frank set pressed tightly against her chest.

Maybe it would be best to just sit it on Maggie's desk before she got there, Evie thought.

However, Evie stopped short in the door of the classroom. There stood Maggie at Mrs. Morgan's desk. Maggie was holding her book bag open in front of her. Mrs. Morgan was sliding what looked to be a Lisa Frank kit inside of it.

Mrs. Morgan locked eyes with Evie for a moment. Maggie turned to Evie and just as quickly looked away. Mrs. Morgan hurriedly zipped Maggie's bag shut.

Evie went to her seat, as though she hadn't seen a thing. She put her replacement Lisa Frank set inside her desk. She wasn't sure what to do. Still give it to Maggie? Take it home? Argue with Meme she wasn't lying, that Mrs. Morgan already got Maggie another set?

Evie stashed her set inside her desk. She figured she'd shove it under books and worksheets. She'd pile her desk so full of papers she could barely close the top and hope, underneath it all, the Lisa Frank kit would disappear. She imagined a black hole would form in the bottom of her desk to suck all those colorful creatures into oblivion.

Evie went about her day of classwork, lunch, and recess. Then, she remembered desk cleaning days. These were days Mrs. Morgan would drag the wastebasket through the class from student to student. She'd go through the mess in each kid's desk, un-ball wrinkled paper. Mrs. Morgan would say, "These were to go home. You need to get organized. What grade are you in? Do you need to go back to kindergarten?" What would Mrs. Morgan do at the sight of the Lisa Frank kit? And the chance of forming a black hole was slim. Evie decided she had to take the kit home to Meme and let Meme decide what to do with it. So, at the end of the day, when the kids got their jackets from the cubby and waited for the bus call, Evie stashed the kit into her backpack.

Nothing seemed off about the dim, early spring day, fit for a light jacket. The sky was gray, like it would rain. The bus ride home was ordinary. The brakes hissed and the driver pulled the big lever to open the doors as she dropped the kids off at their stops. Evie was well ready for hers.

Off the bus, it was a short walk down the dirt road of the trailer court, since Meme and Evie lived in the back. In sight of their trailer, Evie could see Meme hanging the wash on the line. Evie felt all the worse. Meme must have used her laundromat money on the Lisa Frank kit.

The wind picked up something fierce. The sheets blew around Meme. The sky rumbled and sharply turned dark. Oh, how strange. The sky broke loose. Pellets of hail, like little glass beads, pelted little Evie in the face. They rolled like pearls over Evie's jacket.

Evie hurried along to Meme.

Meme dashed onto the porch, waving Evie on, as the bits of hail bounced off the grass.

"Don't see that every day," Meme said. She guided Evie up the steps by her shoulders. As Evie turned on the porch, Meme unzipped Evie's backpack, while it was still on her back. This was something Meme often did.

"What on earth!" Meme said.

Evie realized Meme saw the Lisa Frank set.

"Mrs. Morgan got Maggie another one. I didn't know what to do, so I brought it back," Evie said.

"Well, we'll have to figure something out to make it right," Meme said.

Evie slipped her arms out of the straps of her book bag. She glanced back at Meme. Meme had her eyes fixed on the Lisa Frank folder, which was halfway out the top of the bag.

Another round of hail clunked hard against the tin roof of the trailer.

"Lisa Frank," Meme said, reading out the logo. "If she only knew what she let loose on the world."

Evie knew Meme was talking about Evie's scuffle with Maggie, but she thought Meme, just the same, could have been talking about the hail.

Evie turned back to the hail that spit like bullets. She stepped to the banister of the porch. Oh, what a splendid thing the hail was! It would have Evie raising her hand, nearly out of her seat during science the next day to tell Mrs. Morgan what she saw.

"I saw it too," Mrs. Morgan said.

Mrs. Morgan talked about the hail as a weather anomaly as Evie pondered the image of the earth on the physical science workbook cover.

"An anomaly is something out of the ordinary," Mrs. Morgan said.

Evie repeated the word to herself. *Anomaly*.

"There are exceptions to the order of the cosmos," Mrs. Morgan said.

To Evie, this was more interesting than Lisa Frank ever was.

UNSPOKEN

On that cold October evening, you sat in your lounge chair with your head cocked. Your flannel night dress rested over your body in the glow of the television light. You watched the evening news. The report broke through the static of the antenna. It caught your attention, as it did mine.

I sat near you on the sofa. I had some college applications and financial aid forms on a book in my lap. I had big dreams of going to a school in the city, but I couldn't get past my name on the forms. Really, I couldn't get past our tax form. Dad's layoff at the brickyard. A family of three. Gross income, twelve thousand a year. We couldn't afford college after all, and I didn't see a way I could swing it on my own.

On TV, mobs of queer activists marched with rainbow flags in protest of Matthew Shepard's murder. They were proof there was gay life elsewhere, outside of our little, backwards town. To think entire communities existed, were bold enough to take to city streets. College, I was sure, was the gateway to this world I had longed for. What kind of life would I have if I stayed here? Laid off from some go-nowhere labor job like dad? Living with the shameful secret I was gay?

The newsman said Matthew Shepard, after his terrible attack, had died.

I waited for a sound from you. Your eyes widened with his recap of the events of Shepard's murder:

Tortured.

Tied to a fence.

Pistol-whipped.

By the time the newsman reached *left for dead*, your mouth hung wide open. Your head, I noticed, shook lightly at the newsman's words, *openly gay*.

When he said *hate crime*, you settled back into your seat. After all, this was something that happened far away to a person, in a place we didn't know.

"Awful," I said breathlessly. I hoped maybe you'd speak your mind. Dad was out. It was just the two of us in the comfort of our own home, and Shepard was the first man I heard referred to as *openly gay*.

You didn't respond though. And I lost track of my applications. They slipped from my hands loosely onto my lap.

Though, I should have expected you to remain silent. You had a history of it. Never a word when dad scolded me on how I ought not to sit. Not a word when our cousin's father got furious when I played dolls with the girls. Never a word when I screamed too shrill, playing Indian to cowboys as a child. "Quit screaming like a faggot," the boys said, popping their cap guns into the sky. It was the first time I was called that word.

Is it true what they say, a mother always knows?

Just like then, you quietly stared off into the distance. When the kids ran in front of the bench where you sat on the playground, it was as though it played out, just like the news of Matthew Shepard's murder. No different than something on a TV with a hazy reception, like there was nothing you could do about it. Your silence disowned me.

I looked for something to arouse in you besides discomfort. The last time *it* happened, we sat in Wednesday evening worship in our little church, the Pentecostal Full Gospel Tabernacle. The pastor had placed the loudspeaker in the window. It was directed toward two men staying in the bed and breakfast next to the church. The fire-and-brimstone of Leviticus 20:13 cut through the thick soup of August air and the buzz of cicadas, aimed straight for the two men.

"If a man lies with a man as with a woman, both have committed an abomination; they shall both be put to death. Their blood is upon them."

What was their crime? They were two visitors to our quaint little town. Men, so it was rumored, who shared a single room with a double bed.

I watched you spin the top button of your blush-pink church dress, as though it were a knob that shut off your voice. You sat like the blank, gray, glass, cold screen of a turned-off TV. Surely, you knew the pastor, just as well, spoke of your son.

It was before the news of Matthew Shepard, before *openly gay* was broadcast across our living room. Surely the congregation knew the same softness in me. I grew up with them, after all. Yet the church folk howled like a pack of wild dogs. My own dad sat on the edge of his seat and waved his hanky. "Preach it, brother. Come on now. Tell the Truth now," he cried out.

The minister spit his sermon into the microphone. He raced in front of the pews, soaked in sweat. Your head dropped to your button with the daggers in his words: "Adam and Eve, not Adam and Steve" and "Faggots will split Hell wide open."

That night when the pastor asked for prayer requests, you raised your hand, finally piped-up. You said *"unspoken"* for it was something we held so deep; you dared not say. Yet you and I both knew just who your unspoken prayer request was for.

The power of the unspoken weighed on me as I sunk deep into the sofa. I imagined the parade of rainbow flags, the mobs of queers in the city streets, protesting Shepard's murder. *Couldn't you see there were places I belonged?* I pretended to fall asleep there on the couch after the news. I mourned Shepard. My heart was heavy for him. I imagined his young face from the news, which I found to be quite beautiful. I dreamed we met and fell in love.

You shut off the TV. You took the application that, by then, had fallen loosely beside me. I felt your warm hand brush softly against my arm. I had forgotten after all, how warm that touch could be. Then, you left the room.

The next morning, I found you had laid the applications out on the kitchen table. They were organized beneath a ballpoint pen. The chair was slid back, like an invitation to sit.

With your back turned, you made eggs and bacon on the stove. When you sat my breakfast on the table, you said, "You'll make your way in the world." You sat quietly. You twirled the string at the top of your nightgown while I completed the applications. I signed them and sealed them in an envelope. Though *it* would always remain unspoken between us, I knew exactly what you meant about making my way in the world. Sure enough, I did.

I'd survive somewhere between the memory of Matthew Shepard and everything unspoken between us. I'd sling back shots in bars. I'd wait for the longing stares, the head nod signals of random men and follow them into bathroom stalls. I'd leave straight out the exit after the hook-ups that happened without so much as a look in the eye, never to see or speak to them again. I'd survive, ignoring your calls, swallow through the awkward silence, the pause of your voice in voicemail while you say, "Just checking in. OK. Give me call." I mean, really, what I would say to you when everything left unspoken between us says it all.

NEIGHBOR BOYS

Bruce stands over me in the grass across the street at the old Pearson place. There's a *for sale* sign in their yard. Bruce shows me the flat, black rocks he has folded in his shirt like a pouch. He lifts a shard up to my eyes between his finger and his thumb.

"No, not like that," Bruce says, comparing his rocks to mine. "See mine here, the edges are sharp."

The rock looks just like mine, I think, though I don't say it.

I chuck it. I run my fingers through the grass to find another.

"These are for sure Mr. Pearson's skull," Bruce says.

Bruce has been trying to convince me that Mr. Pearson shot Mrs. Pearson. He says Pearson, then, blew out his brains with a gun on the sidewalk. But I know the Pearsons just moved away. With my own two eyes, I watched both Mr. and Mrs. Pearson, from my porch, load up a U-Haul and drive off. I remember when they left because I felt sad for my mom and dad. They used to do things with the Pearsons. Bruce's parents too. They were losing their friends. Not long after the Pearsons moved away, my mom went to stay with my grandma all the way in West Virginia.

Bruce likes to fib. If I ever argue the truth, Bruce gets mad. I just go along with him. Sometimes, though, it's hard with Bruce to figure out what's true and what's not. He's told me Santa and the Easter Bunny aren't real. He's told me that girls pee sitting down. He's told me that Evil Knievel and Waylon Jennings were Siamese twins separated at birth. If Bruce tells me something, I check it with an adult. Last word from my dad, Santa and the Easter Bunny *are* real, girls *do* pee sitting down (though I'm not sure how), and Knievel and Waylon are *not* even related.

For the Pearson shooting, my dad says that's a flat out lie. Then my dad says, let's talk about something else and acts sort of odd.

Bruce lives right next door to me. Even though he's bossy, I learn a lot from Bruce. He's in third. I'm in first. Bruce can add double digits. Plus, he has one hundred cable channels at his house. I only got three on the rabbit ears. My mom, well, when she's home, only lets me watch PBS, mostly *Mr. Rogers*, when it doesn't cut into her soaps.

"Won't you be my neighbor," I sing out at the thought of Mr. Rogers.

"That shit's for babies. There's better shows. Ones with cars blowing up and shooting with guns. There's even other stuff," Bruce says.

"Yeah?" I asked. It seems as though asking is what Bruce always wants me to do.

"Yeah, I'll show you later," Bruce says. Then, he gets one of his big smiles.

"OK," I say.

Though I don't care to know more, Bruce keeps talking.

"The other night, I snuck down the stairs and peeked around the corner. My mom was doing a puzzle book. She was drinking a beer. My dad was watching something bad on TV. He was drinking too."

"What was he watching?" I ask. I think whatever it is, it must be a big deal. Better than shooting.

Bruce talks a lot about shows with shooting, though my dad says those shows aren't fit for kids.

"A naked lady bouncing up and down on a man's wiener," Bruce says.

"Yeah," I say. I think, why would she do that?

"You know what it's called, a lady bouncing on a man?"

"No."

"Fuckin'," Bruce says. He stands up and puts another shard in his hand. "It makes a slapping sound. The lady says, 'fuck me' and the guy says, 'Oh, baby.'"

"Oh," I say, but I still can't picture such a thing.

"Boys, come in. It's getting late," Bruce's mom, Mrs. B, calls from across the road.

I'd rather go home, but since my mom left, I stay with Bruce while my dad works late shifts at the mill. Lately, my dad's been pulling doubles. Sometimes he even sleeps in the lot in his truck. Saves on gas, he says.

I remember how mom stomped off the porch the day she left. "You want to go off messing with Becky Pearson, you don't need me here to play house! See how you make it on your own. Take care of your son alone," she said.

Messing around, I think. That's like horseplay that gets *you* in trouble.

Bruce and I pile our handfuls of rocks, well, to Bruce, the bits of Mr. Pearson's skull, on the sidewalk.

"We'll come back tomorrow," Bruce says.

Bruce's mom is a good-enough cook. She makes pancakes for dinner. She puts whipped cream on top and that makes them feel special. After we eat, she cleans up in the kitchen. Bruce and I watch some of his shooting shows in the living room. I don't see the big deal. I don't pay them any mind. I find a Spiderman coloring book to keep busy. Except, a man in the show points his gun. It goes off and a lady falls to the ground. This catches my eye.

"Yup. For sure. That's how Pearson did it," Bruce says.

It still upsets me to hear him say this. I go ask Mrs. B about the Pearsons. I wonder if she'll say the same thing as my dad.

"Bruce," she says. "Quit your fibbing or I'll turn off your shows."

Then she looks at me and says, "Now, honey, you know that's not true. The Pearsons moved. You watched them leave, didn't you?"

"Yes," I say.

"Bruce gets big ideas from his stupid shows," Mrs. B says.

Bruce calls me a tattle when I go back into the living room. It doesn't bother me. I think it's good he gets caught in his lies.

On the show, after the man shoots the woman, the police come. A bunch of them.

"So, if Pearson shot his wife, why didn't we ever see any police come around?" I ask.

"Shut up," Bruce says.

I know he knows I'm right.

My mom calls around eight o'clock every night. When she does, I listen in while she and Mrs. B talk.

"Well, you've got to come home, Mary," I hear Mrs. B say. "You've proven your point. The boy needs a mother."

Then, Mrs. B calls me to the phone.

"You being good for Mrs. B?" my mom asks.

"Yes," I say.

"You getting washed up every night?"

"Yes," I say.

"Do you wash your ears good? Under your armpits? Your butt?"

"Yes," I say to all, even though it's been three days since I took a bath.

"You being good for your father?"

"Yeah," I say. "When he's around."

"Figures," she says.

"Listen. You stay away from the Pearson place. And don't go repeating Bruce," my mom says. Her voice goes near a whisper. "He lies. Has a foul mouth like his father. It ought to be washed out with soap."

"When you coming home, Mom?" I ask.

She gets quiet. Then she says, "I don't know."

• • •

That night, Mrs. B puts me and Bruce both in the tub. Around that time, Mr. B gets home from the mill. (My dad says Mr. B's worked there longer and gets a better shift). Mrs. B lets us play boats in the water a while. Mrs. B sits on the toilet. She puts her feet on the radiator and paints her toenails. Bruce has two plain boats at his house. I have one I brought from home. It's a pirate ship with a little captain at the steer. I don't like for Bruce to touch it for fear he'll snap the captain off. When Bruce tries to take my boat, I yank it back and splash water.

"Bruce. That's his boat. Leave him alone," Mrs. B says.

After the water gets cold, we get out of the tub. Then, Mrs. B dries us. She sends us up to bed in clean pajamas. I nearly fall asleep, but Bruce shakes me by the shoulder. He puts his finger in front of his mouth.

"Shhh," he says and waves me on.

We sneak downstairs and peek around the corner into the living room. Sure enough, there's Mrs. B on her recliner with a puzzle book. She sips a beer. And sure enough, there's a naked woman on the TV bouncing on a man.

I can't believe it! It's true what Bruce says that woman does.

Bruce bends over with his arm around his stomach. He tries to keep from laughing out loud. He seems to really like this show.

"Don't know why you watch those movies with fuckin' in 'em," Mrs. B says.

"I like 'em," Mr. B says. Though we can't see him, we hear him on the sofa on the other side of the wall.

But they're gross, I think. I think of that word, fuckin'. I'd be sure never to say that word in front of *my* mom or *my* dad.

"Besides," Mr. B says. "You'd rather have me fuckin' around with Mrs. Pearson, like Fred next door?"

Fred, I think. That's my dad.

"Well, Fred got himself into a hell of a mess. Serves him right, Mary leaving," Mrs. B says. She puts the puzzle book down on her lap.

"Mary needs to come home and take care of her kid," Mr. B says. "The Pearsons moved away on account of the mess. Mary needs to let it go."

Mrs. B shakes her head. She grumbles. Then, she picks up her book.

What they say about my mom and dad makes me sad. I run back up the stairs. Just imagine my dad doing something like that with Mrs. Pearson. No wonder my mom ran off.

I get in bed. I put my head under the covers. I try to keep from crying.

I hear Mrs. B yell at Bruce. Seems she's caught him at the bottom of the stairs.

• • •

The next morning, Bruce wants to go back over to the Pearson's to find more rocks. I tell him my mom says stay away from there, but he ignores me. Then, Mrs. B says we ought to play outside a while, so we go anyway.

From the Pearson's yard, I think about my house and Bruce's, across the road. They are side by side. They looked the same, really. Narrow. White. Except Bruce's house has the door and front windows wide open. You can see right in. Lately, ours is mostly closed up. Even when my dad is home, he doesn't open the blinds.

"Found another," Bruce says. He picks a shard up from the grass, next to the Pearson's sidewalk. The sidewalk goes flat from the road, right up to the Pearson's front porch.

Bruce holds the rock up to the sky.

"Yup. That's a piece of Mr. Pearson's skull," he says.

I think of just leaving when Bruce says this. I worry, though, if I don't go along, Bruce will make my life hell.

Then, to the tune of *Mr. Rogers's* theme song, Bruce sings, "Fuck-fuck-fuck-fuck-fuck-fuck."

I try to ignore him, but Bruce won't let up. I can't hold my tongue.

"My mom says you have a foul mouth like your dad. You both need a bar of soap, she says," I tell Bruce.

"Well, once I heard my dad say your mom's too skinny. He said Mrs. Pearson had a nice, big arse. Your mom's is flat."

"He did?"

"Yeah," Bruce says.

My mom and Bruce's dad always seemed friendly, smiled, and waved hi. I'm surprised to hear he was talking bad about her flat arse.

I want to change the subject, before I get mad.

"I saw a show on PBS one time," I tell Bruce. "A bunch of men went through the dirt with toothbrushes. They found a really old skull, all cracked into bits, and put it back together. You think we could fit Mr. Pearson's skull back together, Bruce?"

Bruce doesn't answer me at first. He does that sometimes. Then, he says, "You know what my mom said when my dad mentioned Mrs. Pearson's arse? She said, 'Well, Fred shouldn't have been fuckin' Mrs. Pearson.'"

I sit up on my knees in the grass. I fake a laugh, cause I think Bruce just likes to see me all worked up. But then, I get a lump in my throat. I feel a drop in my stomach. I can't help but think of that show Mr. B watches. I think of Mrs. Pearson naked, bouncing on my dad. I remember what I heard Mr. and Mrs. B talking about from the stairs. That's true. It bugs me worse than Bruce's lie.

"My mom told my dad, that's why Mr. Pearson shot Mrs. Pearson, then blew out his brains," Bruce says. He points his finger in the air. He stands tall. "Mr. Pearson shot Mrs. Pearson after he found out about your dad, right up there in the bedroom," Bruce says. He points up to the Pearson's window above the porch.

I don't know what to say. I think I might cry. I hold my breath.

Then Bruce walks down the sidewalk. His finger is pointed like a gun. He stomps to his words. "Pearson came down the stairs. Walked out of the house." Bruce stops. He looks straight ahead. "He was standing right here when—" Bruce put his finger above his ear. "BOOM, he blew off his head!"

At "BOOM, he blew off his head," Bruce tosses the handful of rocks up into the air. I curl into my knees. The shards rain down on me and fall against my skull. I keep my face between my legs. I start to cry.

"You OK?" Bruce asks me, though he sounds like he might laugh.

He pulls my arm, but I keep it tight around my knees.

"I'm OK," I choke out. "I think I just got a rock in my eye."

"Let me see," Bruce says. He pushes me over; his face nearly touches mine. He pries open my eye. He looks so deep inside; I can feel his lashes over mine. "It's OK. You're OK," Bruce says.

Then, he pokes his fingers into my ribs. The hard tickle makes me laugh, but it hurts. I roll away, but Bruce pins me down in the grass. I fear I'll never get away from him. Thank goodness, Mrs. B calls "dinner" from across the road. When she calls "dinner" a second time, Bruce jumps up off me with a sing-songy *OK*.

He runs past the *for sale* sign in the Pearson's' yard.

Something comes over me. I pick up a rock. Not a shard—this one's a chunk of gravel about the size of a quarter. I chuck it. It hits the back of Bruce's head.

Bruce stops and grabs his head. He turns around with wide, wet eyes.

"Serves you right, Bruce," I say. I'm surprised when I say it.

Bruce looks shocked. He pants and starts to cry. Then, he runs home across the road.

That night, Mrs. B calls for me a few more times. I ignore her.

"Bruce is fine. It's just a nick. Things happen with tempers. Come in when you're ready," she says. Then, she goes back into the house.

It gets late. The sun goes red. The sky turns pink and blue. It makes an orange glow over our houses across the road. I look at mine, all shut up. Then, at Bruce's. Mrs. B closes the window. Then, the drapes. I wonder what they're doing without me. Maybe eating pancakes? But I still don't go over to Bruce's place. I stand from the grass. I walk over the shards scattered across the Pearson's walk. They crunch and break beneath my feet. Midway down the walk, I look back to the Pearson's place. It's narrow and white, with the same glow from the sun. The windows are all clear of blinds and open. There's nothing left in the house. Then, I look back at the houses across the road. They all look sad. I think I might head to my house, but I can't stand the thought of being alone. Just about then, Mrs. B sticks her head out the door with the phone on its cord by her ear.

"Your mom's on the phone," she says.

I run to Bruce's house. Just in the door, I hear Mrs. B say, "He's usually no bother. Not at all. But I think it's all getting to him. Mary, you've got to come home. Wait. He's here."

I pick up the phone.

"What have you done to Bruce?" she asks.

I start to cry hard while I talk. I can hardly get my breath.

"Slow down, now. Shh. Shh," Mom says.

"Bruce keeps telling lies that Mr. Pearson shot Mrs. Pearson, then blew off his own head."

"Well, you know that's a big story. Now, don't you?" Mom says.

"Yeah, but—" I say. "Then I heard Mr. B say Dad and Mrs. Pearson were—fuck . . . I mean, doing something bad," I say. "That's why the Pearsons left."

The phone goes quiet for a bit. Then, my mom says, "Well, we'll always hear stories. It's the truth that really hurts us."

That night, Bruce lays on the couch with a cloth on his head.

Mrs. B says, "Aww, come on now Bruce, it's barely a nick."

I watch him from the kitchen doorway. He doesn't look at me. He doesn't say a word.

Mrs. B calls us into the bathroom. Bruce has his arms folded and ignores me as we go through the door. It hurts to stand next to him, knowing he's mad. Something comes over me a second time that day, but it's to make things right.

"Bruce," I say. "I'm sorry." Then, I reach for the basket of bath toys between the tub and the door. I pull out the pirate ship. "Here. You can play with it," I tell Bruce.

Bruce looks at me and smiles. He holds the ship in his arm.

"That's good friends, making up," Mrs. B says.

She runs the bath. She yanks at my pants which always seem to get stuck at the heel.

"See it?" Bruce asks. He points at the nick on his head and pushes his hair out of the way with his finger.

To be honest, I can barely spot the cut, but I play it up. "Oh man," I say, like it's bad. "What's it like, getting hit by a rock?" I ask.

"Not that bad," Bruce says. "Not like a stabbing movie I was watching."

"Stabbing?"

"Oh yeah. A lady stabbed a man. There was blood everywhere."

"Tell me more," I say.

While Bruce talks about the movie, I think about my parents. When I see my dad, I'll tell him to say sorry to my mom. I'll tell him I threw a rock at Bruce. I said sorry, and now we're getting along just fine.

A SON WITHOUT COMPASSION

Jeff zips off the exit toward home. He's wracked with visions of his mother's rickety house on the hillside. It's the sore thumb of the block. Not the Wal-Mart, John Deere version of nice. Not the neighbors' tidy two story, vinyl-sided houses. They all have hanging baskets of geraniums, pristine grass, and pinwheels blowing in flower beds of petunias. Jeff's mom's yard is overgrown and full of junk.

It's twenty more minutes of travel and dread to Clearview, the little rust belt town where Jeff's mom lives. When he arrives, he parks his car on his mom's street. He gets a good look at the place. It looms over Jeff like a monster. It's worse every visit. Always more stuff. It's hard to believe how things have gone downhill since Jeff's dad died, especially since Jeff's dad was a handyman who kept things tidy. Sadly, he had a heart attack in front of his work shed in the side yard when Jeff was just seven years old.

Straight out of the car, Jeff notices how his dad's work shed has caved in the center. The roof lays over its trusses like a wet blanket. Next to the shed, the riding mower sticks out of a big hole in a weathered tarp. It's seized up in the grass. The grass is knee-high around it. It reminds Jeff of a gallery crawl he recently attended in Pittsburgh. One of the exhibits titled *The Futility of Life* had a black and white photo of rusty old cars that were bumper-to-bumper, like a traffic jam in a forest.

On the house porch, there's also a sofa under a tarp. It surfaced a few years back, shortly after Jeff moved out. Jeff's mother says she loves the retro floral print on it. She says she wants to get the living room cleared out before she brings it inside, but the sofa has to be dry rotted by now. Can't apply logic though, Jeff reminds himself. The sofa's piled high with a mountain of junk, what Jeff's mom calls her thrift store treasures. There are shelves to a bookcase, a walker, a tire that might fit her car (nearly like new, she says). There are bags of clothes, bins of pots and pans. There's another bin of toys, mostly old He-Man action figures. Jeff's mom says they're hot ticket collectibles and folks on eBay would pay top dollar for them. She just has to figure out how to list them on the site. All the junk blocks the living room window behind it, and it's been shut up for years. Jeff's mother started to bring random shit home shortly after his dad passed. She plays up its usefulness, what she will do with it, but never does anything. This has only gotten worse over time, and by now, she's a full-fledged hoarder.

Jeff takes a deep breath up the steps that lead to the porch, looking over all the junk. Jeff hasn't been home in four months, even though it's only three hours from Pittsburgh, where he now lives. Jeff steps into the yard with his hand over his eyes to block out the sun. He inspects the roof. A large chunk of tar paper has blown off the front corner. As he looks up, he steps to his right to get a better look. Jeff stumbles backward over a stroller in the yard. "God damn it," he curses. He just catches his balance before he falls down the steep hill. Most of the old tar paper is cracked and rippling off the roof. A good storm, and it'll be gone. Jeff's patched the roof to hell and back, but it all needs to be completely redone. Too bad Jeff's mom doesn't have money. She lives off his dad's survivor benefits. She says she gets some other money from Social Security, but Jeff's not entirely sure for what. Maybe for being crazy? Maybe for her bad back?

Even though Jeff feels defeated, he's determined to patch the worst spot on the roof. He's purchased the stuff to repair it, and he hopes the tarpaper hasn't gotten ruined in the shed. The house is a money pit. Jeff certainly doesn't have the cash to fix it. He's a dishwasher at Chili's and barely gets by. Jeff moved to Pittsburgh for culinary school after high school. However, he dropped out in his second term. He might re-enroll. Cooking has always been his thing. It's the tests he can't pass. Plus, the line cook and three of the waiters at Chili's are distinguished alum, which doesn't say much for the degree.

Jeff's mom sticks her head out the front door. She smiles and says, "Jeffie" to greet him. She is a hummingbird of a woman, just shy of fifty, with a pixie cut. She steps onto the porch. She has on a dress over pants—a mix match of polka dots and stripes, an ensemble that really completes the package. Jeff imagines a runway voice-over for his mom, Cindy. *In this versatile number, Cindy breezes from her days feeding stray cats to romantic evenings sifting through the neighbors' trash.* Jeff can't help but laugh. That's only funny for a moment though. Probably because of what happened to his dad, Jeff fears his mom could drop dead any day.

"Should I be expecting a sibling?" Jeff asks. He turns. He gives the stroller a nudge with his boot. It rolls a bit across the yard. "Damn near killed myself on the thing. You need to get rid of it."

"No, sir. I just picked that up from a yard sale. Five bucks. You never know when someone will need one. You know what those cost new?" Jeff's mom asks. She picks up the lid of a tin garbage can on the porch, where she stores dried cat food. She pulls out a handful.

No arguing with the woman, Jeff thinks. He watches his mom toss the cat food onto the grass, like one would toss bird seed. The cats, mostly feral strays that have gravitated to his mother's house over the years and multiplied, appear from the junk in the yard. Three cats crawl from the cluttered sofa on the porch. They give a big yawn and stretch. They scurry off the porch for the food in the grass. It's competitive eating. Their little sharp teeth crunch up the dried bits of food.

"If I can keep the rain out, I can get this place in shape," Jeff's mom says. She reaches back into the can. Then, she tosses another handful of cat food.

"I don't know, Mom," Jeff says. "That roof is bad."

I call bullshit, is what Jeff really thinks. Fixing the leaks won't change a thing. He'd never say it right out, even if it's God's truth, though. So, Jeff gets one of his dad's old ladders from between the fence and shed, the same spot where Jeff's dad left them the day he died. He gets tar paper, a bucket of tar, a hammer, and nails from the shed. Luckily none of the supplies has gotten too damaged, in spite of a hole in the center of its roof.

"I call spotter," Jeff's mom says.

She sounds like a kid playing a game. This reminds Jeff of how she was when he was growing up. He, more so, saw his mom as a playmate.

She always had a thing about aliens, and she and Jeff would search the night sky for UFOs. She had Jeff convinced every jet, every star, every blip in the sky was an extraterrestrial sighting. Sure, he believed all the stuff when he was little. Then, around age eight, after his dad died, Jeff decided all the alien stuff was a bunch of bull, because . . . it was. He would still go along with it though, since it seemed important to his mom. Then, around age ten or eleven, it just got annoying. Seemed it was all his mom ever talked about, almost manically. Jeff would say, "Mom. I think that's just a plane. Mom, I think that's just a star," to steer her off the topic. Then, she'd argue with him. "No. It's not," she'd say and fabricate something odd about the lights traveling across the sky. However, Jeff saw nothing out of the ordinary, just the standard issue American jet.

Finally, one day, Jeff had enough. On the porch, Jeff's mom came out with her binoculars to search for UFOs. Jeff bluntly said he was tired of hearing about alien crap. Jeff's mom stormed into the house. Jeff could hear her inside. It sounded like she was crying. After that, she never mentioned anything about aliens or space again. Jeff tried to apologize. He even said he saw a strange orange light in the sky, but his mother just shrugged him off.

Around the same time, the other kids on the block asked Jeff, "What's with your mom?" Seemed they noticed she was a little off too. Jeff made it a point to hang out at other kids' houses. That way, he didn't have to defend his mom's odd behaviors to them. Besides, his friends' parents always seemed to like taking Jeff on. Jeff milked every bit of their sympathy. He always looked like he was having the time of his life in his friend's clean, wall-to-wall carpeted houses. He'd tell his mom not to pick him up after little league practice in her old Chevette. The car was cluttered, rusty, and reeked like gas fumes. Instead, Jeff would soak up the air conditioning in his friends' parents' minivans. Most evenings, he'd bail on Coco Puffs for dinner out on the porch steps at home. Instead, he'd head to his friend's houses. He'd splash in their above ground pools while their dads barbequed at the grill. Deep down, though, Jeff felt awful for ditching his ma. So just as his friends made plans for sleepovers, Jeff would head home. Always, even if he had to walk alone in the dark, even if his friends couldn't understand why.

As Jeff climbs the ladder, his mom talks to one of her cats. Jeff looks down at her.

"What are we going to do, Scruffy? Why don't you get up there and help Jeffie?" she asks as she stands with her hands on her hips in that get-up of hers.

The cat circles her ankles. Jeff can't help but laugh endearingly at her. He shakes his head.

Aside from his nerves on the pitchy roof, the repair goes smoothly. It only takes about an hour. Jeff heads down the ladder with the tar bucket, hammer, and nails, when he hears a "whoo-hoo."

Jeff looks over his shoulder. His mom puts her finger to her mouth, pantomiming a gag. "Eugenia," his mom mouths. Then she rolls her eyes.

Jeff's mom and the neighbor Eugenia Yarger have been at war over the state of her place for years. There've been several fines from the township for property code violations. The complaints are all anonymous. Jeff's just as sure as his mom that Eugenia's the source. Part of Jeff wishes Eugenia would back off, but then again, he feels bad for Eugenia. She has to live next to the eyesore, after all.

If it wouldn't look obvious, Jeff would climb back up the ladder to avoid Eugenia. Instead, he keeps going down it. He steps off the last rung, firm on the ground, as his mom and Eugenia greet each other. The way they say each other's names is civil at the surface, but it takes on the undertone of two rival Aztec warriors. If it weren't for small-town, Christian values, Jeff's sure, one would sacrifice the other by ripping out her heart.

"Look what the cat dragged in," Eugenia says. She stands at the edge of her perfectly cut property line where Jeff's mom's grass nearly reaches her knees. "God bless you. God bless you for helping out your momma. You're a good boy, Jeffrey. Good, indeed. Mom's blessed to have you. You do what you can. Lord knows. How long you in for?"

"Ah, he's alright," Jeff's mom says. She crinkles her nose and swats her hand in the air.

"Thanks, Ma," Jeff says. "I'm just in for the day," he tells Eugenia.

Jeff's mom puts her hands on her hips. She keeps her back to Eugenia.

Eugenia wears a pink, plaid housedress. Her hair is rolled tight to her scalp in her usual Saturday curlers. She's prepping that hair volume for

Sunday worship where she plays piano up the street at the First United Methodist. Jesus, Jeff thinks, you've never heard a meaner rendition of *Up from the Grave He Arose*. Then he thinks, shit, Eugenia looks just as crazy as his mom.

"That's a shame," Eugenia says. "There's so much to do."

Jeff's quick to turn away from Eugenia and his mom. The way Eugenia's words land, he's sure, they're about to square off.

"Oh, here we go," Jeff's mom says, turning to Eugenia. "It's always the same old, same old with you. Now, what's your problem?"

"Jeffie's more than welcome to use our mower. I'm worried about snakes in this high grass. Maybe you can get some of that rubbish off the porch too. That's a rodent's paradise."

"I got cats, Eugenia! Cats! You're worried about snakes. Rodents. But you called the township on me because I have too many cats!"

Jeff walks away toward the shed, glad he's got a can of tar to put back.

Eugenia ignores Jeff's mom. She speaks to Jeff as he walks away. "God bless you, Jeffrey. You know if you ever need a decent place to stay when you're in, we've got a spare room."

"That's mighty kind of you, Ms. Eugenia," Jeff says without missing a step, without looking back, without meaning a bit of it. "But I've got work tomorrow."

"Well, aren't you the giver. You operating an orphanage for grown men with moms?" Jeff hears his mother ask Eugenia.

Jeff keeps going for the shed.

The women really lay into each other.

In the shed, Jeff looks through the hole in the sagging roof, up into the blue sky. Eugenia's dig (and Jeff's sure that's what it is) about a place to stay really bothers him. Lord knows, that's why he day trips. He hasn't set foot in his mom's house for two years on account of the condition inside. It's something he and his mom have never talked about. There are plenty of places in town where Jeff could crash, for sure, but not a single one is home. Truth is, Jeff has scheduling preference at Chili's. He's off every Sunday and Monday, but he'll never tell a soul back home.

When it gets quiet, Jeff peeks his head out of the shed. He sees Eugenia storm off. His mom's on the porch opening a new tarp out of its package.

"Help me put this up," Jeff's mom says. She stretches the tarp open in her arms and holds it up to the side of the porch facing Eugenia's. "Maybe this will block Eugenia out."

Jeff helps his mom put up the tarp.

Later that evening, Jeff and his mom pull into the lot of the Clearview diner. Besides pizza, it's the only place to grab a bite in town.

In the car, Jeff's mom pulls an aerosol deodorant from her purse. She sprays her pits before they go inside. Then, she hands it to Jeff, like it's good pot or something, like hey, you want a hit?

They both laugh.

"Get your feminine antiperspirant out of here," Jeff says. He holds his breath from the smell.

"Hey, it's magnolia blossom," Jeff's mom says, as she gets out of the car. "You should be crawling out of your skin to smell like one."

Jeff and his mom walk down the narrow aisle of the diner. It's the usual cast of home perms and overalls. The townies seem to all pause for a moment at the sight of Jeff and his mom. They're quick, though, to steer their eyes away from the town crazy, at least with Jeff looking out behind her. He imagines the whispers behind their backs. *Go ahead. I dare you to say a word,* Jeff thinks as he peruses the diners.

Jeff and his mom take their seats. She puts her hand softly on his arm. She doesn't say anything when she does this, but Jeff takes the gesture like, hey, it's good to see you, son.

She tells the waitress, who looks like a high school kid, "Better be good grub. You're serving America's next top chef, you know."

Jeff is embarrassed. He's never told his mom he's dropped out of culinary school. When his mother asks him about his classes, he says they're fine. Nothing to really talk about. He's quick to move on to other things.

Jeff's frustration from the day seems to fade at his mother's touch. He feels the weight of every time she's told him he's the love of her life. Being with her, for a moment, at least, feels good. However, Jeff would give a million dollars if she had someone else to dote on. Maybe a handsome, genius little brother. Hell, even a burn-out boyfriend with a loud motorcycle would do, if it meant there was someone to share the burden of her.

Jeff decides to bring up the house, just after the waitress serves their sandwiches and fries.

"What do you think a new roof costs?" Jeff asks. He reaches for the salt and pepper. "I'm sure, more than you and I have put together."

Jeff's mom swats her hand in the air, like she's shooing off flies.

"Ever think about selling? The house would be a great fixer-upper for a young family in town. You could probably even turn a little profit. Find something more manageable, like a nice little apartment," Jeff says.

"Pssst. Yeah right. And what about all my stuff? Besides, who'd take care of all the cats?"

Jeff wants to ask how many cats, in the past year, his mom has scooped up off the street with a shovel or found bloated, dead out back. He's sure Eugenia Yarger's husband has been poisoning them, since Eugenia complains they piss on her porch. To boot, Eugenia's husband once told Jeff that antifreeze and canned tuna was a sure recipe to get rid of pesky cats. Unfortunately, there's never been any sure proof of this, and Jeff can think of two or three other people on the block capable of such a horrible thing.

"How many cats do you have now?" he asks.

"I'm down to nine," Jeff's mom says. "Thanks to Eugenia and her husband. If I ever get proof. Besides, the house is worth something. When I die, you can sell the place to pay for my funeral," Jeff's mom says as she eyes up her cheesesteak. She uses both hands to close the bun and lifts it to her mouth.

Jeff's speechless. He watches his mom bite into her cheesesteak. Onions fall from the end of it onto her plate.

Jeff takes a bite of his own buffalo chicken sandwich.

"Did I tell you?" Jeff's mom says with a mouthful. "So, I'm sleeping in my chair in the living room, and I wake up to this crinkling sound, like plastic wrappers." She places her sandwich on her plate. She wiggles her hands in front of her mouth like a critter. "There he was in the corner of the living room. A raccoon. His eyes glowing. You know how their eyes glow at night, Jeffie? That little bugger stole a box of my Little Debbie brownies. Even the cats are just looking—you know the way the cats' ears sort of perk up, like, man, who's this weird looking cat, right?"

She puts her fingers to the top of her head like cat ears, and she wiggles them. "I call the raccoon Brownie. Ah Jeff, he's the cutest thing," she says. She covers her mouth with her hand as she chuckles.

Jeff realizes he's frozen mid bite. His eyes feel wide.

Jeff swallows hard and says, "Doesn't sound safe. Where you think it's coming in?"

Jeff figures once they get back to the house, he'll look in the cellar, find the hole, and block it. He hates to admit it, but Eugenia's right about the rubbish attracting varmints.

"Who knows," she says with a shrug. "Besides, Brownie's harmless. He's welcome to come and go as he pleases." She takes another big bite of her cheesesteak.

Jeff hasn't seen his mom this giddy in some time. Not since her excesses on UFOs.

After dinner, Jeff drops his mom off at the house before he heads to Pittsburgh. He tries to shake off the idea of his mom squatting in the living room with a raccoon. But he doesn't look into it. It's *her* house, and she's perfectly fine with it.

Jeff kisses her goodbye. He feels the tickle of peach fuzz on her cheek when he does.

• • •

Jeff can never call his mom. The landline has long been out. She has a government funded cell, but unless she's on it, she keeps it turned off. No matter how many times Jeff has shown her how to check her voicemail, she swears she can't remember how. It's become a running joke. This comes up again during her routine eight o'clock Sunday evening phone call with Jeff. Jeff's a pacer on the phone—well, at least when he talks to his mom. She asks Jeff again how to access her voicemail. She says she's expecting an important call from Social Security for a benefits review.

"There's a little envelope icon at the top of the screen on your phone," Jeff says as he swipes the dirty clothes on the floor by his bed out of the way with his foot.

"OK," Jeff's mom says. "Let me get a pen and pad to write this down."

Jeff hears his mom riffle around the house.

"Where the hell are all my pens?" she asks aloud.

Jeff hears drawers, things falling, his mother sifting through papers. She lists random things she comes across in her search.

"Oh, there's my tennis bracelet. Just needs a clasp. I thought I lost it when it broke. Cool, my *mammogram, be sure and get yours* water bottle from the health bazar at the medical center. I wondered where I put that. You know, I have pink lawn flamingos here. I found them in Mrs. Mayhue's garbage when her kids cleaned out her house after she croaked. Can you believe it? I found three. I think they're the originals. These things sell online for twenty bucks a pop . . . Aw, Jeff. It's a picture of you in your little league uniform, when you were eight, maybe nine. I remember the time you struck out and cried. So, after the game, I took you for ice cream at Scoops. Remember that?"

"I don't remember that" Jeff says. "At all."

"You were playing that team in blue and gray. What was that team?"

"I don't know," Jeff says in frustration, given his mom's inability to stay focused on her voicemail, thinking of all the one's he's left in vain. "My voicemails to you are probably floating in the galaxy somewhere."

As soon as this escapes Jeff's mouth, he regrets his poor choice of the galaxy for a point of reference. Ever since the UFO debacle, Jeff's been sure not to reference anything related to aliens or the universe or space.

Then, Jeff's mom says, "Tell you what, you yell a message into the sky later. I'll tell you what I hear, after it makes its way across the galaxy."

After Jeff hangs up the phone, he actually sticks his head out the open window of his apartment. He yells, "You're nuts, woman" into the night sky.

The next time Jeff talks to his mom, he asks, "Did you get my message?" He clears an ashtray and beer cans off the sticky, carved-up coffee table in his apartment.

"Now, Jeffie. You know I can't figure out my voicemail," she says.

"No. I mean, the one I yelled out into the sky."

"Jeffie! You didn't do that, really? Na," she says. She laughs. "Oh wait, hold on a minute. I didn't get it directly, but I intercepted it from the aliens. They say, 'Jeff, you're the one who's nuts!'"

Jeff's not sure whether he should be amused or horrified. He's both. On top of the alien reference, he wonders, *What are the chances she'd come back with a similar message?*

"Oh, did I mention . . ." Jeff's mom segues. "I've been feeding Brownie chips. Right out of my hand."

Jeff hears that spark in his mother's voice, the one he saw in her eyes when she first mentioned Brownie. This makes Jeff worry he's opened Pandora's box.

"Mom, you shouldn't be messin' with that varmint."

"Varmint! I'll have you know; Brownie is a class-act raccoon. Only varmint around here's that two-legged snake next door, Eugenia. She called the township on me again. The code guy said if I don't get the yard cleaned up in a month, it's another hundred-dollar fine."

Jeff thinks of how many fines his mother's racked up. She says the magistrate only has her pay ten dollars a month based on her modest income. Jeff can't help but think, as the fines mount, she's got to be near a lien on the property.

He almost brings it up, but instead, there's an awkward silence between him and his mom and—

"Earth to Jeffie," she says. Jeff imagines his mom cupping her hand around her mouth, miming a loudspeaker.

Jeff's certain she'll go down the rabbit hole with the alien thing, like when he was eight. *What should he do? What should he do?*

"Shoot," Jeff says. "I got another call coming through. Probably work. I better go. Love you, Ma." But Jeff can feel his mom linger on the line. "I'll see when I can come in to help with the yard."

Jeff stacks his own dominoes. He thinks over his schedule. He wonders how he'll find the money for gas or the time.

"Hey, thanks," Jeff's mom says. "Love you. Bye."

. . .

Jeff and some friends go clubbing on a Saturday night in downtown Pittsburgh. The stage lights flash red, blue, yellow, and green in sync to the thumping base of dance music. A pretty brunette chats Jeff up at the bar. He buys her a beer. When she asks what Jeff does, he tells her he's a dishwasher at Chili's. She says she has to go to the bathroom; she'll be right back. Jeff's eager to keep talking. However, when the girl walks out of the women's room, she goes straight to the other end of the bar. It's as though the two had never met. It's a slight brush with romance, something that, at twenty-one, Jeff has never, ever gotten too near. He can't help but think she ditched him because he's just a dishwasher. It's a hard taste of people's hang-ups. The Bacardi and Cokes go down smooth until two a.m. Jeff wakes with an *oh shit* in the morning. He flies into Chili's twenty minutes late for his shift. He realizes early into his shift he still has a buzz. He can smell the cigarette smoke and the booze coming out of his own pores on the dish line. He grows nauseous, as the day wears on. He gets some aspirin from the office, and he drinks Cokes to ward off a full-on hangover.

Jeff takes a spatula off the edge of the counter to wash. Ginny, the sorry old biddy who works the grill, the type of downer everyone on shift sort of works around, goes apeshit on him. Jeff's not sure why. There are at least three others hanging clean on the rack in front of her face.

"What's it there for? Good luck?" Jeff asks. He puts the spatula right back in the same spot. *How can someone be so uptight?* he wonders.

When Jeff takes his break, Ginny's in the breakroom. She lines up a fork and knife and a Diet Sprite. She bites into her plain chicken sandwich (just a patty on a bun). She peers over her glasses to read a gossip rag in her usual spot. It's as though everything she does implies, *mine, mine, mine.* Ginny's a life of order and misery. Jeff considers, at least, there's a loving freeness with his mom, even if she's a mess.

Jeff sticks his head out the door for a smoke, making sure to steer clear of Ginny.

Jeff's cell phone rings. Eugenia Yarger's number comes up on the ID. God damn! Eugenia's made Jeff's number the complaint line for his mom. Eugenia usually starts her calls with words like *heartbreaking, worry,* and *Christian duty.* This is the version of Eugenia who sends over warm meals to his mother in Tupperware she'll never get back. However, it's just a matter of time before the complaints start. This is the other version of Eugenia. The one who always has an angle, the one who keeps calling the township on Jeff's mom. Jeff jumps at the opportunity to put Eugenia on speakerphone in the breakroom. He expects, like last time, his coworkers will gather around, bent-over, stifling laughter while Eugenia prays in her pitchy voice to *the Lord Jesus in Heaven for little Jeffie and his momma*.

"It's Eugenia," Jeff calls out to his friends Destiny and Jake who are within earshot in the kitchen.

They rush to the door smiling.

"Sweet," Jake says.

But when Jeff answers, Eugenia gets right to it.

"Jeffie. When are you coming home? For Christ's sake. Your mom's really lost it."

This is a first. Eugenia's angry toward Jeff. Her tone conjures up the image of someone hurling stones. Jeff notices Destiny and Jake stall in the door. Their mouths gape wide open.

Jeff's amiss with his usual go-to which is, "There isn't a whole lot I can do." He's not sure what it is, exactly, Eugenia's getting at.

"You need to stop making excuses," Eugenia says.

Jeff can feel his stomach sink. His heart races. He swallows. Eugenia's stones hit pretty hard.

"And you don't even know it, Jeffie. You don't even know it. Poor thing's been wandering around town all hours of the night with a stroller," Eugenia says.

"What—" Jeff starts to ask.

"A stroller, with who knows what in it! Probably a dead rat!"

It's then that Jeff blows his stack with the biggest line of mother F-, cock-sucking, mind your own goddamn business, that's ever come out of his mouth. However, Eugenia gets the last word, and man, it's one hell of a blow.

"You know what you are. You . . ." she says, "are a son without compassion."

"Compassion?" Jeff yells. "You know everything I've done for my mom—"

Jeff hears a click and the dead tone of the receiver.

Destiny and Jake cover their mouths.

Destiny asks, "Jeff, are you alright?"

At the same time, Ginny peeks over the top of her gossip rag with a scowl.

"What the fuck are you looking at?" Jeff asks Ginny.

Jeff feels dreadful and out-of-sorts for the rest of his shift, as he scrapes bits of food from plates into the garbage bin and hoses ketchup from the serving trays. It helps him a bit to apologize to Ginny, even though she shrugs and tightens her lips when Jeff does this.

• • •

Jeff heads for Clearview at four o'clock straight from his shift, still in his stained red Chili's shirt with the pepper logo on the front. The evening summer air whips through the car window as he zips down the highway. He sips a Mountain Dew and gnaws away at a box of Little Debbie Nutty Bars. His mom is heavy on his mind. The thing about the stroller? Why? As the cars flash by, he thinks over his last phone conversation with his mom. She said she hadn't seen Brownie. Jeff can't shake the idea that she ended up scraping Brownie from the road with a shovel, maybe after he was hit by a car. He envisions his mom singing lullabies to a dead raccoon that's bundled up in a baby blanket. Jeff's convinced, after years of walking the line, his mom's finally gone over the edge. Damn, Eugenia's right. Something needs done.

When Jeff rolls into town, he's the only car on the road. He makes the ascent down the hill-of-a-street home. He passes Eugenia's house with a big F-you. His tire rim scrapes the curb as he pulls near the sidewalk in front of his mom's. By then, it's night. The headlights beam up the hill. The cats scurry across the lawn. As Jeff gets out of the car, he sees his mom in the soft glow of the porch light. She's fussing with the stroller.

"Jeffie," she calls out as she gets up.

Jeff hears the surprise in her voice, but Jeff walks around the car without saying hi.

"Mom, you gotta listen," Jeff says as he charges up the steps.

His mother steps back and furrows her brow.

"Eugenia called," Jeff says. "Something about you out all hours with a stroller."

"Well, when did you and Eugenia become pen pals?" Jeff's mom asks. She folds her arms and wags her head from side-to-side.

"Hear me out. Answer me," Jeff says.

She doesn't answer.

"Mom. Mom. You can't be doing that. People already think you're nuts."

"What about it? Like I care what people think," she says.

Jeff steps past his mom. He peers inside the stroller. Thank God, there's no roadkill. In fact, there's nothing inside.

Jeff lets out a man-are-you-crazy laugh.

Jeff turns to his mom. She stands near the house door. She opens it and waves Jeff in with a let-me-prove-something grin.

She's really soft with the door. She hunches low when it opens. She hushes Jeff, who thinks it's been two years since he's crossed that threshold. He braces himself for a good look at it. He stifles his breath when hit with the shut-up, cat piss smell of the house.

For the first time, Jeff sees it, really sees it. The moon casts a light over piles of rubbish. The floor's only cleared enough for the door to swing. From there, it's completely covered. The junk looks a foot deep in places. The abandoned items of everyday life lie like ruins, like every hope and dream, Jeff figures, his mom has ever had. In the corner, there's a pile of clothes next to his mother's reclining chair. On top of the clothes pile, the glow of three little sets of eyes strike Jeff.

He hears the crinkling sound of snack cake wrappers.

"Brownie's not a *he* and Brownie has a brood," Jeff's mom says. Jeff can't quite see his mom's face, but he hears her exhale.

"I haven't seen Brownie for three days. She'd never leave her little ones behind. I take *them* out in the stroller at night, thinking maybe, just maybe—"

Jeff's mom steps through the room, like Moses parting the waters. She picks up one of the raccoons. She finds footing in the rubbish and lurches to hand it to Jeff. Jeff gasps at the sight of the little raccoon's curious face. Its paws rest over his mom's hands. Its feet dangle in the air below its plump belly. Jeff reaches out for the little critter. Its little paws wrap around Jeff's finger. Jeff draws it into his chest. It's a tiny thing and feels like a squishy softball, warm and soft against Jeff's chest. It can't be more than a few weeks old.

Then, Jeff's mom hands him the other two. He struggles to keep them in his arms, but they grab onto his shirt. They yank his hair as they climb up him like he's a jungle gym. He fumbles to keep control of them.

"Maybe she's gone to find another place for them because we're—," Jeff stops himself. "You're handling them."

"For three days, Jeffie," his mom says. "Think about it. She would have just moved them. No. Something's up with Brownie."

That night, Jeff and his mom—it's her idea—take the little raccoons out in the stroller. Jeff tries to talk her out of it, at first, but what she says makes sense, possibly, at least.

"Maybe if she's lost somewhere or trapped, she'll track their scent," Jeff's mom says.

Jeff's sure there'll be talk tomorrow of the town crazy and her wacka-doo son, but the two walk around town. Jeff's mom pushes with the stroller while Jeff rubs little Debbie plastic wrappers together and shakes a box of snack cakes. They yell, "Brownie! Here Brownie!" Let them all think what they want, Jeff decides. The years of hiding it, trying to manage it all—it lifts, at least for the time being. *Who cares what others think?* Jeff asks himself.

The night is so vibrant. The navy sky is crisp with so many stars. The streets are quiet. Jeff feels like he and his mom and those little raccoons in the stroller, with the sound of its wheels rolling across the pavement, are the only strange beings to cross a vast galaxy.

But a little way down the road, Jeff sees lights cross the sky. Jeff's first instinct is to point out everything ordinary about the aircraft. He's nearly ready to explain why it isn't a UFO, but he stops himself. In fact, Jeff sees something odd about the shape that makes it seem unusual, not like the standard jet.

Then, as Jeff looks away from the sky, *it* comes towards them . . . the thrilling sight of two glowing eyes.

WE BURY OUR OWN

We've still to dig Pap's grave, and his old Ford dump truck won't start.

Joey's head's under the hood with a wrench, trying to get a stripped damned bolt out of the starter.

A horn honks.

Joey jumps and damn near knocks his head.

I look outside the garage door.

It's Mrs. Mayhue with her daughter in a Buick Skylark.

Mrs. Mayhue's in babushka. She waves her arm out the passenger window.

That horn honks again.

I head toward the garage door.

"Old neb-shit, sniffing around," Joey says, without looking up.

It's freezing cold. The driveway's a sheet of ice from the storm last night. I walk slowly. I stay close to the old junk cars on the side of the driveway, so I have something to grab onto, lest I fall. I'm no kid myself at fifty-five. Last thing I need is to crack my skull. End up dead in the snow like Pap.

I reach the car window.

Mrs. Mayhue holds a covered dish in her hands.

The smell of meatloaf wafts out of the car.

Mrs. Mayhue wears those thick, old glasses that make the eyes look big. With her sharp nose, they give her the likeness of a bird. She peers up at me through the fog on her lenses.

Mrs. Mayhue, a long-time widow, came around asking for Pap after Maw died in '79. She brings over pies—cherry, raspberry, blueberry.

Sometimes, banana bread or homemade melt-in-your-mouth buns. That's fine. But, what's not so nice . . . She barks orders around *our* house. She has me and Joey scrub the kitchen floor on our hands and knees. She stands with her fists on her big hips while we clean. Her voice sticks in my head like a plague. *Why would you grease monkeys wear your work boots into the house? Sit on the furniture in a scruffy old work suit? Lay in a bed all filthy dirty without so much as washing up, brushing your teeth, or combing your hair?*

Mrs. Mayhue lifts the dish to the edge of the car window. "Hard to believe Pap seemed right as rain the other day," she says.

When she says this, I picture Pap the way Joey and I found him. Flat on his back by a shovel in the yard, gray-blue skin, dead in the snow.

"Sure is," I say and choke back the sorrow. "Damned coot! Snuck out at the crack of dawn to shovel before we were up."

"Eighty-on. Shoveling snow. With a bad heart," Mrs. Mayhue says, shaking her head.

The smoke rolls from the muffler of the car, and the fumes blow over me with a gust of wind when she says this.

Mrs. Mayhue's lard-ass, snooty daughter picks her nails in the driver's seat. She glances up at me, but doesn't say a word, like I ain't even a person worth the talkin' to.

"What are you poor fellas to do out here in the middle of nowhere without Pap looking after ya?" Mrs. Mayhue asks.

"We'll manage," I say.

Mrs. Mayhue looks away. "I pray," she says. "I'll be lost without your Pap. We were the last of the Mohicans."

If there was anything romantic between Pap and Mrs. Mayhue, I don't want to know about it. I do know they'd sit at the kitchen table and talk into the wee hours about the old days. They went to church and school in the little chapel where we'll bury Pap, some four miles deep down a back, country road.

I take the dish.

"It's the least I can do," she says.

Mrs. Mayhue's the old-fashioned type who wears a dress, no matter how cold. She reaches for a plastic bag on the car floor between her legs. The bare skin of them shows between her skirt and the top of her boots.

"I brought you some dress pants and shirts that belonged to my husband. They should fit you. You'll get all washed up for the funeral, you will. Pap would want it. And remember the chapel is the house of the Lord. If you were to go see President Reagan or some big star like Conway Twitty, you would get gussied up. You'll look your best, you will."

Like I'd go see either of them, I argue to myself.

Mrs. Mayhue dangles the bag out the window then plops it on top of the dish.

Now, I'm put off by the idea of wearing a dead man's clothes. If I had more gumption, I'd say, *That's kind of you, but we have good clean flannels and jeans of our own to wear tomorrow to Pap's funeral. Of course we'll wash up, woman.* Instead, I say "Yes, ma'am."

"I'll be out to the funeral tomorrow, I will. Lord permitting. Who knows, my age, it may be the last time I set foot in the old chapel," Mrs. Mayhue says. She pulls a balled-up hanky from her coat pocket and wipes her nose. A tear streams from the rim of her glasses down her cheek. She wipes it away. "Well, my heart goes out to ya," Mrs. Mayhue says. Then, she clears her throat.

"We're sick over Pap," I say. "Thank you kindly for the food."

"You digging the grave today?" Mrs. Mayhue asks.

"Yes, ma'am," I say. "Once the truck is running. Joey's working on 'er now."

"Oh, the keys!" Mrs. Mayhue says. Then, she reaches for her purse. "You'll want to go to the chapel early to get that old pot belly stove fired up," she says. "God knows how long it will take to get it stoked in this cold."

She rifles through her purse, and things jangle while she sweeps her hand down to the bottom. She lets out an, "Oh," then, "Wait a minute. Wait a minute." Then, she lifts out a key on a worn, blue ribbon. "Can't forget that," she says.

She hands me the key.

Mrs. Mayhue's daughter puts her hand on the gear shift and idles the gas feed.

"Now hear me. Put on those good clothes tomorrow," Mrs. Mayhue says. "It means a lot to look good, it does."

"Yes, ma'am," I say, as I stuff the key in the waist pocket of my overalls. Her daughter shifts into drive and the car juts forward a bit.

"Oh, have you got flowers?" Mrs. Mayhue asks.

"No, ma'am," I say. "We ran out of money."

Mrs. Mayhue shakes her head. "I think I have silks at home. I'll bring 'em. If there's anything else you need, you call on me, you hear?"

"Yes, ma'am," I say.

Then Mrs. Mayhue nods.

Her daughter takes off before Mrs. Mahue's window's up.

A squall of snow blows across the fields. The taillights fade out of view.

When I get back in the garage, Joey holds up the starter in his hands.

"That's half the battle. I got one better for you," I say.

I sit the meatloaf on the workbench. I pull a pair of pants from the bag, which are some polyester shit. I put them in front of me and shake 'em around. I move my hips like Elvis or some shit, trying to give Joey a little laugh, since he looks to be on his last nerve. "Mrs. Mayhue says we're to wear these dress clothes from her dead husband to the service tomorrow."

Joey doesn't crack a smile. "My ass," he says.

It takes about five more hours from the time Mrs. Mahyue leaves to rebuild the starter. We sand the rust off the bolts and bits, then put them all back together again. We sort out what goes where with what.

I wished we had the money to go to Auto Parts to buy a new starter kit, but the last bit of money we had from tearing down an old trailer and hauling it for scrap left us five hundred dollars. We made good with the undertaker for it.

Once the starter is mounted fast, we have an extra bolt or two.

Joey looks up and says, "If you think this is funny, Pap, It's not."

Pap always goofed around with us when we worked. He'd say, "Hey there's a naked lady over there in the woods," or "Shit, there goes a bear," or "You smell a skunk?" Me and Joey might look or jump. Pap would bend over, hold his gut, and laugh. He'd say, "You boys are hella gullible. I gecha' every damn time!"

I have a penchant for getting irritated easy. Joey too. And I'd say, "son of a bitch" or Joey might throw down his shovel when Pap cut up. The angrier we got, though, the more Pap would laugh. The more he'd laugh, the more we'd ease up.

It's a nerve-wracking thing, losing time on the truck. At least the funeral arrangements are taken care of. For years, the undertaker's known Pap. Pap was a gravedigger all his life. He buried most folks in these parts. The undertaker gave us a fine oak casket instead of pine on account of this, and he isn't charging extra to bring Pap's body all the way out to the chapel in the cut. It's a haul from town with the hearse, in the bitter freeze at that. Hardly a plow or salt truck goes through these parts. The roads are sure to be all ice. Damned near treacherous. Makes me wonder if a hearse has four-wheel drive. I imagine pushing a hearse that's spinning in the ice somewhere along the road with poor Pap's corpse in the back.

"Help us, Lord. In everything we do," I say under my breath.

It's the funeral Pap wanted. It's the least we can do. A quick blessing in the chapel. Closed casket. Then, to be buried next to Maw by Joey and me. Pap taught us everything we know, even if other folks didn't see any worth in us. They'd call us Frick and Frack growing up. Now, mostly, just the two old scruffs. But hell, Pap always said, "Pay 'em no mind. The Lord looks at the heart." Just the thought of his voice saying it brings tears to my eyes.

The kerosene heater is kicking in the garage. We drink Coors to calm the nerves. We chew snuff and spit it in jars. Limbaugh's on the talk radio, yammering about Dems taking our guns. We eat the meatloaf straight out of the pan.

I bite it close to my hands. Taste a bit of motor grease from my hand on my tongue.

"Hallelujah," Joey shouts when he gets those last few bolts on the starter. "Give 'er crank," he says.

I jump in the driver's seat and turn the key. The engine grinds and coughs a bit. Then I lay heavy on the gas. It revs.

We fill the truck up with diesel and back 'er out of the garage. Let 'er idle in the drive. She chugs out black smoke.

While the truck idles, we get ready in the house. We layer up in thermal. We put on our work suits and Carhartt jackets, knit caps under hoods. We tie the hoods tight against the ears. We put on wool-lined, suede work gloves and double up layers of woolen socks. We yank on the thick-padded Arctic Cat boots Pap bought us last Christmas. Then, we fetch the shovels and picks and such from the shed.

"Pap would have us bury him in the cold," I tell Joey as we get in the truck.

Joey shakes his head. "Keeps you from going soft," he says.

We pull out of our little house. I catch the light in the window of the house in the rearview mirror. The line of the roof slopes under the sky. The old asphalt siding has half fallen off, and in spots, the old, weathered wood planks show through the walls. The junk in the yard peeks through the snow. The light shines white at the top of the garage, a big, two-port, metal building that dwarfs the house.

We head off for the chapel, a left-over place from the old farming village The way out is all woods now. Never strip-mined, like most of these parts. A couple of empty shacks dot the snowy road. The gray treetops hang over it, weighed low with ice. We pass McClaren's old barn. It's caved in at the roof and looks like spilled matchsticks sticking up from the snow. There's the odd trailer or little place still occupied. Someone's son or grandson, still on the land. But the old timers, like Pap, are mostly all gone.

Our tires, nearly bald, spin on the slick roads. The diesel chugs, and puffs out black smoke as we go along. I think of how this road was when we were kids. Men on tractors would wave hi, stop in the middle of the road. Pap would hang out the truck window, and they'd bullshit a while. Not like today. Seems you know of people, but you don't know 'em anymore. Folks nearly run a fellow off the road, zipping by in souped-up trucks. Worse, I'm afraid to talk to half of 'em. All you hear about is meth going around anymore. I fear stopping for someone along the road. I hear some people faked a broken-down car a while back, then beat a fellow who stopped to lend a hand, robbed 'em blind, left 'em for dead.

"Get us there, Lord, and get us back home," I pray to myself, with the way the roads are, the way the truck grinds along.

We pass the trailer where Donahue's boy lives, shacked-up with a Milliorn girl. They have two dogs, maybe some Rottweiler part something, on a long run. The run goes between their trailer and their shed, next to the road. The dogs bark and zip across the run. They snap at the leash and bark and snarl as we pass 'em by.

"Poor old dogs," I say.

Joey says, "Ought to leash the owners out there a while in the cold. See how they get along."

Seeing the dogs out the side mirror as we pass 'em, and with memories heavy on the mind, I think of our old German Shepherd, Roscoe, from when we were young. Pap kept him snug on an old, braided rug next to the coal burner when it was cold. Maw would say, "Pap, you do that dog better than your boys." Pap would say, "Sure, and they'd put me out, just the same, for old Roscoe." Joey and I would laugh. This was true. We all loved that dog.

It's near four o'clock when we pull up to the chapel lot. It's covered in snow, so we park just off the road. The sun's a blaze of orange as it breaks through the gray, winter sky. It swells in its last hour, and bursts into colors of blue, pink, and gold through the clouds behind the chapel's little steeple. The hues of it glimmer on the glossy snow, like a fine selenite stone. It's a pretty sight, really.

I can just envision us kids, like ghosts, out in the cemetery around the chapel, playing tag like we did after Sunday school. It's been some time since I've been out here. It's mostly like I remember, except most of the tall old elms in the yard are gone.

Just a step out of the truck, the winds whip over the cemetery bluffs. The bone-chilling cold. Twenty's the high. Night nips with the lows.

We get the tools from the bed of the truck. With picks and shovels over our shoulders, we crunch through the frozen snow, 'neath the dusting on top. It lies in mounds where the headstones line the cemetery. Our feet break through with each step, and we cave into the snow up to the knees, and the crunching sound it makes is amplified with the jacket hood tight against the ears.

Straight away, the wind stings the bare cheeks. They go numb.

Our trail of craters leads to Maw and Pap's headstone on the family plot.

Seems like yesterday Maw passed, but hell, it was some ten years ago. I can remember me and Joey begging Pap at the chapel door to let us help with her grave. But Pap wouldn't budge. "No man should bury his mother," he said with tears misting his old blue eyes. *No man should bury his wife*, I thought, but Pap had that look of a man who's been stripped of all he has. I feared he might just sock me in the mouth if I said it though. So, Joey and I sat idle at the repast under a canopy next to the chapel, pushing around potato salad on foam plates along with the family that came to pay respects for Maw. Pap buried Maw alone.

Joey and I plunge our spades into the snow. We make our way to the earth. A few shovels in, sweat settles under the shirt. There's no way to avoid it, and once the body's wet, there's no chance to fight off the cold.

Joey and I fetch a cord of wood and a bent-up tire rim from the bed of the truck. We clear a spot next to the grave. We stuff the rim with the wood and old bits of paper. We snap twigs from the trees. They make a sharp sound in the tight, winter air.

I block the wind with my body, while Joey lights the paper. But the wind spits up another squall. Our little flame is snuffed out.

I look around the woods and the cemetery yard as Joey tries to light a flame. There's no sign of life about. It feels lonely, left out in the cold. I long for the caw of crows in the treetops, a snap of a doe in the brush, a squirrel barking on a high branch to claim his turf. But nothing stirs. Nature's no fool, I think. Not like *man* out here. But, then again, I reckon man's the only creature to bury his own.

Joey slips his hands out of his gloves. I squat over the sticks to better block the wind. A paper catches. We nurse it with more paper and twigs until it takes off. The flame grows, cracks loud. Its embers defy the cold.

By the time we clear the snow from the grave, the sun sets low. Night bleeds blue. We set our picks to the earth. We break through the sod to the clay below. Strange digging a grave without Pap looking on. I envision Pap by his headstone telling us, "Be sure it's square, level, six feet up."

"Remember our first grave?" I ask Joey.

"Roscoe," he says.

"Yup," I say. "God, we were just boys." That old dog was our third brother, I swear. Raised 'em from a pup. I remember the day we found Roscoe dying, old. He laid quivering on his side, smelled of the piss that soaked his hind. Flies gathered on his eyes while he lingered there on his rug.

"We stayed by him for hours till he passed," Joey says.

"First ever I saw Pap cry," I say.

"I remember that shovel being just as tall as I was," Joey says, standing. He lays his spade hard into the ground, digs his heel on its step.

"Near kills a man, burying your own," I say.

"Sure 'nuff," Joey says. He pries a shovel full of earth from the ground.

It's two feet in until the earth is no longer frozen.

The fire crackles high in the air, as we work at a breakneck speed.

The mucky clay clings to the shovel. We bang the spade on rock to set it loose.

Nearly four feet in, the sky goes navy, dotted with stars. A full winter's moon shines bright. I can see the glow of its atmosphere.

The flame lights Joey's face orange while he digs under the stars.

He unzips his coat.

I stall from digging, catch my breath, and take a look at the white stars.

I feel like I'm playing out. I put effort to keep steam with Joey, who digs steady and hard.

I hear the dogs howl in the distance. Sounds like a cry, weary, sad, and low. I reckon it's the dogs chained out on the run.

"Think they cry from the cold or just howl at the moon?" I ask Joey, as I unload a shovel full of dirt.

"Just doing what nature's bred them to do, I reckon," Joey says. He pauses and wipes his brow.

I howl out, just like the dogs.

Joey shakes his head, let's out a huff.

The dogs reply.

The sting gets in my fingers and toes. My toes curl in my boots. I press my fingers tight against my palms inside my gloves.

Even Joey breaks for a while. He takes his gloves off and puts his hands near the fire to warm.

It's two more hours of digging. The brown earth is piled next to the grave and dusted in the snow. We jump down in the dark grave with flashlights and our picks and shovels to square it off. It's slick with puddles on the bottom, and the boots slosh loud in the mud.

When the grave is square, we hoist ourselves back up to the ground.

I buckle at the knees and kick with my boots against the clay earth. It smears across the knees of my work suit.

We tip the embers from the old tire rim down in the hole.

We take our tools to the truck and load them in the bed.

"I can't wait to get home, curl up in bed," I tell Joey, with a yawn. I reckon I'll lay there and think of Pap in the wee hours though. I don't plan for much sleep, just warmth and the comfort of home, however sad a place it is with Pap gone.

"Yup," Joey says.

We get in the truck.

Joey turns the key.

The ignition cranks, but, son of a bitch, she doesn't turn.

"If it can go wrong, it will," I say.

"God damn," Joey says.

He tries starting the old truck up again, but she grinds and grinds. Then, she just makes a clicking sound. Joey flicks the headlights. They gleam through the thick frost on the windshield.

I crank the heater knob. It just blows cold.

With the body settled down from work, I catch a terrible chill. I shiver. My teeth chatter hard.

Joey pops the hood.

We jump out of the cab. We take our gloves off to open the hood latch and fiddle with the starter. The starter is like a block of ice, and the fingers stick to the metal. The connections are sure. Joey tells me to give 'er a crank, but when I do, it ticks with no juice kicking through.

Joey kicks the bumper and throws his hat in the snow.

I get in the truck, close the door. Take shelter from the wind, at least.

Joey gets back in too.

"Ain't worth losing time on the truck. No chance of anyone coming along some icy night on these roads," Joey says.

"Maybe we set foot up the road to Donahue's trailer," I say.

"I dunno. He was never too friendly, and I heard he did time for some mess. Besides, by the time we'd get up there we'd be nipped with frostbite, near losing our toes," Joey says.

I picture the Donahue boy looking like some junkie with a shotgun at his door. I imagine those Rottweilers set loose on our heels.

"Key!" I say, as it comes to mind.

I rise in my seat. I unzip my coat, the front of my work jumper. I dig in my jean pocket, not sure I left 'em in there.

"Key?" Joey asks.

"To the chapel," I say.

I yank out the key. It dangles on the ribbon like a precious thing.

"Mrs. Mayhue dropped off the key to the chapel, so we could get the furnace set in the morning."

Joey shakes his head and breathes out hard. He falls back in his seat. "Thank God," he says.

We're quick out of the truck. I fumble with the keys at the wooden chapel door. I have to pee, which makes the fumbling with the tight lock feel longer, worse. The door is red, which shows to the eye like burgundy in the moonlight, crackled in years of thick paint. It swings open.

Joey flicks the light switch, just inside the door. The sound of electricity hums in the room, and the lights that hang from the vaulted ceiling pulse dim then brighten as it buzzes through.

The chapel's a little old place built sometime in the mid-1800s with a platform, a pulpit, and an old, upright piano with a dark wood finish. There are no more than ten pews. The old potbelly stove sits in the back with buckets of coal.

I pee outside against the chapel. *God forgive me.* Steam rolls from the piss as it soaks the clapboard.

When I go back inside the chapel, Joey's already got coal in the stove. I pull wads of paper we didn't use for the grave fire from my pockets. I quiver, still desperate to find the lighter. Twice, I search all my pockets and finally find the lighter in my work jumper.

We light the paper and nurse the flame over the coals in the stove. It's forty minutes or so of stoking the flame, until the furnace picks up and starts to warm. We put our hands near the cast iron. At first, it's tolerable, but when the cast iron heats up, we touch our palms against the stove like a game of hot potato. We kick off our Arctic Cat boots. There's a pain when I peel off my socks. My feet are bright red, like blocks of ice to the touch. We hold our feet near the grate of the furnace to thaw them out. They feel damp long before they feel the slightest bit warm. It takes effort to wiggle the toes. When the heat has taken hold, we lay on the pews, still close to the coal burner.

Joey rolls his jacket up for a pillow and puts his arm over his face.

I can't wind down. I walk around the chapel. The floorboards snap like they've come to life, I swear. The warmth brings out the smell of the place. Murphy's soap, old song sheets, and holy oil from the pulpit. I imagine the place as it was. I remember where the Donahues sat, the Mayhues, the Fosters. We sat in the third pew back from the pulpit. Pap always sat on the end of the pew next to the window, next to Maw. Now the place is shut up and still. All the old-timers are gone.

The panes of the window fog as the warm air meets the cold draft. I look out into the night through the foggy glass.

The dogs come to mind. But I don't hear a sound. I hope they've gone in. Not died in the cold.

It's a sad place to be, this little chapel here. I think about it, like I've never thought before. *Who'll paint the clapboard, patch the roof, tune the piano, fire up the stove?* I think to ask Joey if we should tend to the place, but I hear him snore, out cold. *For whom?* then I wonder. I cover my head with my coat until it's all blackness. I imagine how death might feel.

Morning comes quietly. I listen for the dogs when I awake. Seems nothing stirs.

Joey and I tidy up the church. Clear the muck from our boots off the floor. We shovel the lot and a path to the door.

Around eleven fifteen, Mrs. Mayhue and her daughter come in the Skylark, driving slow down the slick road.

Mrs. Mayhue slips her leg out of the car door. She holds a spray of artificial roses, just as she said she'd bring, red and blue.

"You'd best, at least, have your change of clothes," she says, as she hoists herself up in the car door.

"You won't believe the time we've had, stuck out here in the cold," I say.

Mrs. Mayhue's eyes widen. She stalls with her arm over the top of the car door.

"To hell with the clothes," Joey barks. "The Lord looks at the heart."

The tears swell in the corner of my eyes. "The truck died. We were stuck out here. Damn near froze."

"Froze!" Mrs. Mayhue repeats. She steps around the car door. She slams it.

Her daughter comes to her side. They take careful steps across the lot. I look at Joey. He looks at me. We offer them help, take their arms. I take Mrs. Mayhue's arm. Joey takes her daughter's.

"A terrible time you've had. Poor boys," Mrs. Mayhue says, and the way her voice sounds, I envision an old dog gone from a snarl to whimper as it cowers low to the floor.

In the chapel, Mrs. Mayhue sits on a pew with her daughter, handy the furnace. They're quiet. Mrs. Mayhue looks at the ceiling with her hands over her belly. Then, she rubs them over the top of the pew in front of her. She picks up a hymnbook and flips through it. She clears her throat, and the sound owns the room.

The hearse comes thirty minutes late. The undertaker brings along two helpers and the old minister from town.

We men usher Pap's casket across the lot into the church.

We rest his casket on the stand, near the pulpit, and we all gather around it.

The minister reads from the Bible. "Lay not up for yourself treasures upon the earth where moths corrupt, where thieves may steal. But lay up for yourself treasures in heaven. For where your treasure is, there will your heart be also," he says.

He asks Mrs. Mayhue to sing a song.

She says, "This was Pap's favorite gospel tune."

I wonder what it is she'll sing.

Her voice isn't anything pretty. It cracks when she starts. But she stands with her fists bawled up. Tears stream from her eyes. They are closed the whole time she sings. Her voice grows deep. It goes through the rafters of the chapel and right through my chest. I swear it goes right through my soul. It's a song I remember from when we were kids. She sings, *"So let the storms rage high. The dark clouds rise. They won't worry me, for I'm sheltered safe within the arms of God. He walks with me, and none of earth shall harm me. Sheltered safe within the arms of God."*

I cry in heaps.

I see Joey cry.

When Mrs. Mayhue finishes the song, it's as though time has stopped. I stand stunned, like a stranger in my body.

Mrs. Mayhue reaches over the casket and touches her hand on my arm.

I ring my right fist into my eyes.

The minister prays a blessing that the Lord will go with Joey and me in life.

The service ends.

Mrs. Mayhue tells the men about the truck, how we spent the night.

The undertaker and his fellow go with us to the truck to see if they can help.

Joey gets in the driver seat and turns the ignition with the truck key. The damned thing starts!

I think it is something, somehow, Pap has done.

We men take Pap's casket through the snow down to his grave.

"God bless you," the undertaker says after Pap's lowered in the hole, so do his helpers, the minister too.

We walk back to the lot and see them off.

"You go 'head," Mrs. Mayhue says to the men. She turns to Joey and me. "We'll wait here 'til you're done. Be sure to follow you home. God forbid, you'd get stranded again in that old truck," she says.

"Oh, go on," I say. "No use waiting."

"She's running," Joey says. "Should be fine."

Mrs. Mayhue shakes her head and closes the door to the church.

Back at the grave, we pile the dirt gently over Pap's coffin. I look up, see Mrs. Mayhue through the chapel window. She sits next to her daughter, wiping her nose. The sun glows over her. She looks different. Almost pretty, like a figurine inside a pretty box.

I imagine her voice over and over, singing Pap's favorite song. I think of how she knew every word by heart. She's the last of the old-timers. All I can hope is that with Pap gone, she'll still come around.

Two hours to cover, the grave is done.

Joey and I head to the chapel. We haul out the ash and damper the stove. We lock the door. We take the women's arms and walk them to the car.

"Can't thank you enough," I tell Mrs. Mayhue, as I hand her the key. She grips it tight in her hand, beneath the fold of my arm.

"Would you come 'round for supper?" I ask her.

"Can you cook?" she asks.

"I'll figure something out. Get a recipe from one of Maw's old cookbooks," I say.

Mrs. Mayhue looks at her daughter.

Her daughter raises her brow, bites her lip on the side.

"And we'll sit at the table and eat proper in a nice, clean house?" Mrs. Mayhue asks.

"That we will," I say as I help her into the car.

"That would be fine," she says.

In the truck, down the road, I look in the passenger rearview mirror to catch a glimpse of Mrs. Mayhue, as we slowly drive 'round the curves, with Joey careful at the wheel. There's a comfort in seeing her behind us, in the Skylark. She sits with her hands over her plump belly in the passenger seat.

Past the Donahue boy's trailer, Joey pumps the brakes.

Pap's truck skids on the road, pulls me out of my thoughts.

Those Rottweilers are off the leash. They dart from the front of the truck. They're great big dogs up close, and they bark and nip at the tires 'til we lose 'em down the road.

"There go your Rottweilers," Joey says. He has a stern face and a furrow in his brow.

Maybe I'm slap happy, exhausted, near losing it, but Pap's tomfoolery comes to mind. I say, "Joey!"

In his seat, Joey sort of jumps.

"Watch out for a naked lady, a bear, and a skunk."

Joey cracks a little smile.

The truck goes quiet for a good while as we head on down the road.

Joey grinds down the gear. The diesel stack puffs out smoke. Joey says, "Some folks go to funerals. We bury our own."

A GOOD FATHER

Jeb watches his wife Beth in her blue dress and Mennonite head covering. She sits by Esther's hospital bed and caresses the toddler's fingers. Jeb hates to leave her alone in Pittsburgh at the Children's Hospital, but he has to get back to the farm. Jeb's had the church van for two days now. Beth needs a change of clothes. The spring plowing needs done, and Jeb needs to set eyes on the other five kids. All this to do, then Jeb plans to head right back to Pittsburgh in the evening. He and Beth have a meeting with the doctors at five o'clock. Little Esther, shy of two, has Spina Bifida and Hydrocephalus. The doctors have her, all tubes and wires. She's got a fever. They put her in a drug-induced coma. They'll have to make a decision about another surgery to take pressure off the brain. They'd originally planned for just a day at Children's so the doctors could change Esther's shunt. It seems things always go wrong with a shunt. This is Esther's fourth or fifth. Maybe her sixth. Jeb doesn't remember. All the trips back and forth, the days and nights in hospital waiting rooms are a blur. This time, though, seems worse than the others. The doctors say little Esther has sepsis.

It's not so bad at the hospital when Jeb and Beth run into other Mennonites or maybe the Amish in the waiting rooms. Jeb grew up in the Old Order. He converted to Mennonite so he could read the Bible in English for himself. His faith, not order, moves him closer to God. Sometimes, Jeb and Beth talk with the English who are friendly. Anyone there with a sick child knows the same trouble. Beliefs make no difference to that.

As Jeb gets ready to leave, he kisses Beth on the back of the head. He taps little Esther on the foot. He hopes she might miraculously flinch. She doesn't move.

"Sit close to the nurse's station if you have to step out," Jeb tells Beth. Sometimes the nurses will ask Beth to leave the room when they change Esther's tubes. Jeb recalls the time a beggar went through the waiting room and demanded Jeb hand him money, stood close over Jeb and wouldn't stop asking, though Jeb politely said no. Jeb fears a similar intrusion could happen to Beth without him there looking on.

Jeb leaves in the wee hours to avoid traffic. Down the parkway out of the city, his hands cling to the steering wheel like it's life itself. Beth stays on his mind. She's thin and pale. She hardly eats. Jeb doesn't seem to know her anymore. All her life, Beth cares for little Esther. Jeb misses the touch of his wife. He wakes most nights to find her side of the bed empty, and he finds Beth watching over Esther all hours.

Jeb is tired of the doctors messing with little Esther's head. Everything in his heart wants to tell them to stop. But if they let Esther go and she doesn't make it, Jeb wonders if Beth could take the loss. Worse, she would blame him.

A big semi-truck veers around Jeb into the passing lane. Must be going eighty miles an hour. It makes a big gust of air that veers the van into the berm. The van rumbles as Jeb steers it back on course.

As Jeb gets a half hour out of the city, there's less traffic. Jeb's grip loosens on the steering wheel. The sweat of his palms dries up with each mile closer toward home. He longs for little, winding roads.

An hour out, Jeb realizes the van needs fuel. With all the waking hours on his mind and the tired setting in, Jeb stops at a Speedway for coffee and gas. The English woman at the gas station counter is plump in a pink sweatsuit. Her hair is sprayed out like a nest. She wears a bunch of make-up on her face. She chats up a scruffy man. Though the man is balding on top, he still has a long ponytail down his back. When Jeb checks out, the pair look at him funny. Jeb dresses in the old way with blue trousers and suspenders. He keeps a traditional cut and has a long beard. Jeb thinks the couple looks strange. Yet somehow, among the English, he's the one out of place.

Jeb gets back on the road. He sips his hot coffee while he drives. He longs for a few hours of sleep when he returns to the farm. It would feel good to lay in a warm bed, but this can't happen. Once Jeb drops the van off at the church, he'll grab a bite to eat. The other kids should be rising by then. Miriam, his oldest at sixteen, should have breakfast cooking.

Jeb's near the end of his cup, as the road gets familiar. The coffee is like cold spit, but he sucks down the last drop. The little white farmhouses dot the countryside. The sun is setting over the trees. Jeb sees his brothers' farms have already got their plowing done. He thinks, when they see his fields lay untouched, they'll wonder what's gone on with little Esther. They'll come check in, but Jeb will be there plowing. They'll talk about the season. *What do you think of the later frost?* They might complain of plowing mud, but Jeb will say, *Should have a good start on the crops with all this rain. It could be worse. We could plow the muck the old way, with horse and hitch. Not a tractor,* he'll say. And it will be as if things have gone back to normal. But Jeb knows they'll ask about little Esther. It will be real again. *She's not good,* he'll tell them. *Not good at all.*

Jeb pulls into the church. Parks the van. He finds a scratch of paper and a pen in the visor. *Can I take the van around three?* Jeb writes. He wraps the note around the keys. Kind Pastor Fisher is not around yet, so Jeb throws them in the mailbox. He figures the pastor will let him take the van again. Pastor's never said no. However, since the community shares the van, someone else might need it. Jeb worries he puts them all out. Jeb will be sure to tell the pastor he's mighty grateful when he sees him again. He'll have Miriam send a pecan pie from her mother's recipe, since the pastor once said how good it was at a church picnic.

Jeb walks the half mile home from the church. It's a chill outside. In the mid-forties. Jeb closes his coat. He looks at the sky. The fog of morning dims out the sun. It's around six o'clock. Folks should be rising. Looks like a good chance of more rain. Jeb passes Yoder's field. The cows are just let out of the barn. They bite at the damp, spring grass. Jeb hears the sound of his feet crunch in the gravel on the berm and the low mews of the cows in the field. A crisp vapor of breath rolls out of his mouth in the cold. He's quick to walk. Perhaps, his feet race to match his mind. A cold sweat sets in under his jacket. He opens it back up for air. He's short of breath from hurrying along. Not long after, he sees his house, a soft glow of light in the kitchen window. Jeb turns up the long, dirt driveway from the road. Jeb's glad he'll see the other kids. He's only been gone for two days, but Jeb feels it's been a long time. He fears he could walk in the door and the children would all look like strangers. He wouldn't be able to tell little Zack and Job apart. Caleb would be grown into a man. Miriam would be a picture of her mother, cooking in the kitchen in her place. Little Ruth would wonder *who's that man* when she sees Jeb.

Jeb recalls how Beth told him something wasn't right with her pregnancy before Esther's birth. She hadn't gained the weight she did with the other children. She was very tired and struggled through her daily chores. Beth went into labor with Esther early while canning in the kitchen. The midwife said Beth was passing out and losing blood during labor. Jeb thought his wife would die young that day at thirty-five. That day, Jeb ran to the community phone to call the ambulance. The English doctors did good for Beth. They had all these things to help her that the Mennonites did not, and Jeb thought it the Lord's will to get good help. It saved his wife. But Esther? Since the day she was born, she just lays there, barely a sign of life. Jeb hates to think about it, but he wonders if little suffering Esther's life is worth living. If he could go back, when the English doctors first started fussing with Esther's head, he would have said no. Perhaps, she wouldn't have lived. Then, Jeb chastises his thoughts that life might be better had she not made it. He turns them to other things, lest he finds them a sin. And he thinks of his meeting later with Beth and the doctors. His heart longs to say no more shunts, no more operations, no more fussing with Esther. Yet he's not sure he can speak those words. He imagines a look on their faces, if he does, their wide eyes wondering, *What kind of a man would want this?*

Up the drive, every bit of grass on Jeb's plot looks familiar. Jeb has a count of each post on each fence 'round the fields: two hundred and thirty-nine. Everything he passes is touched by his hand. He sprints up the steps to the front door of the house. It's a good feeling. A little moment where Jeb can put his worries aside.

Jeb sees Miriam through the kitchen door, just to his left.

"Father," Miriam says, as she turns from the stove. Jeb hears the delight in her voice, sweet as the smell of maple syrup on the table. She is a good daughter and already at the griddle making breakfast for her brothers and sister. Zack and Job, age six and seven, come down the steps.

They are followed by Caleb, fourteen. Caleb holds little Ruth. Ruth has her arms tight around his neck. Ruth is four. They all come to greet their father. Jeb notices their hair is still on-end. Zack and Job fall into Jeb's waist to hug him. They look up at him. Their eyes are still sleepy. *Little buggers,* Jeb thinks. They are always in cahoots, and Beth often sends them to Jeb for a scolding. Seems twice a week she does this. Jeb tries to be cross with the boys, but they look at him with their big eyes. Seems they like spending time with their father, in spite of the reason. Jeb puts them to work on some tasks. He shows them how to gather hay and how to milk a cow. He tells them to be sober-minded, like the Bible says. "What's that mean?" they ask. "Be serious and hard at work," Jeb explains. They try for a bit, but they always end up carrying on. They push and shove one another instead of sharing their work or taking turns. Jeb can't help but laugh at them, though he tries to hide his smile. Jeb imagines he'll tell Beth what they're up to, how they cause a ruckus back home. She will laugh when he tells her, as though they are a funny story from her past.

The boys ask about their mother and Esther.

"They're still at the hospital," Jeb says. He cannot bear to give them bad news, so he tells them what they already know.

Jeb kneels down into Zack and Job. He kisses them and wipes the sleepers from their eyes. Their breath is fierce.

"Did you brush your teeth?" Jeb asks.

The boys say, yes. Jeb knows it's a lie.

"Do it again," Jeb says. "Your hair needs brushed. Your face needs washed."

The boys run back up the stairs.

Caleb, who now stands eye-to-eye with Jeb, comes to greet his father. When he does, little Ruth leans into her brother's nape away from Jeb. Ruth has a tender heart. She's always fit to cower back, hang her head, and cry. Not to upset her, Jeb ruffles her hair, then leaves her be. He and Caleb head into the kitchen.

"How's Esther?" Caleb asks, as he puts Ruth into her highchair.

"Not well at all. There's a fever and sepsis. They put her in a coma. I have to head back to Pittsburgh for a meeting at five," Jeb tells Caleb.

He knows Miriam hears. She sort of shudders and shakes her head at the griddle.

Jeb can feel the weight of emotion with the children. The doctors have always been frank about Esther's condition. She could die anytime.

Jeb goes over a list of things he's told Caleb to do: mend the fence along the Yoder's field, get the greenhouse cleaned and ready, fix the hinges on the barn door, sagging from winter.

"Yes," Caleb says to all.

Jeb tells him, "You are a good son."

Miriam brings pancakes to the table. Zack and Job come from upstairs. Jeb inspects their faces to see that they have cleaned up properly before he allows them to sit. He tells them, "Good enough," and they sit at the table. They eat up the food. They are all quiet, somber in their ways, like they don't want to disturb their father. Jeb longs for a scuffle between the boys or a fit from Ruth. This would make it like any ordinary day.

"Some brothers have come to plow the fields," Caleb tells Jeb, like it's something he's forgotten. Really, Jeb thinks his oldest son is trying to spare his pride. This is the way of the Mennonite, to help one another in need. Yet, since Esther's birth, Jeb's family has always needed help. He feels he can never live up to the favor. Jeb just nods to Caleb, like that is well. Though, he is hurt. Maybe it's silly, but plowing is something his heart was set on doing. Jeb takes a few more quick bites. Then, he pushes back his chair. The sound it makes seems to startle the room. Jeb tells Miriam what to pack to take back to Beth, that he's going to the field. He tells Caleb to get to the barn. The cattle should have been tended before breakfast. He realizes he's harsh with Caleb, straight away, after all his eldest son has done. Yet he can't linger on it.

Jeb steps out the back door of the house to survey what's been plowed. A large swath in the field just behind the house has yet to be turned over. Jeb heads to the shed for the tractor.

He drives the tractor onto the field toward the unplowed land. The big tires sink into the soft, wet soil. Something about the loose dirt, the plowing done by another, makes Jeb feel like a stranger on his own field. He's done all his farm work single-handedly, since he first moved here, after he married Ruth. He likes to be on the tractor. Not because it's less work. It's mostly where Jeb thinks. Like sitting high, he takes stock of all that God has given him. He sorts out the details of what he must do or rather how God might best use him. Many times, he has a young one or two sitting on his lap. Jeb lets his kids hold the wheel like they're steering the tractor along. They swell with pride believing they can run a tractor. Jeb recalls the smell of a child's soft hair blowing in the wind, how he sneaks in a kiss at the back of the head in the sun. Every child he remembers, Miriam, Caleb, Zack, Job, little Ruth. But as he goes through each memory, he knows he's never done this with Esther. Her limp, little ragdoll body. She's never walked. Never spoken. Never laughed. Never smiled. He thinks this is something he should try, same as the others, but then, he shifts the gear of the plow. The tractor makes a terrible jerk. Oh, it's a foolish thought, to risk a child like that on it. Her little body would slump over. How easily she could topple off. She'd never gleam with the same pride as her brothers and sisters. Then, Jeb thinks of Esther more with regret. Jeb's afraid Esther's a stranger to him. Jeb thinks of the few times he's kissed Esther on the forehead at night, but never the back of the head. And the kiss is not like that with the other children, it seems. If Jeb is honest, each time, it's as though he kisses little Esther goodbye. He's never rocked her or fed her or gotten to know her like the others. Jeb's quick to get both hands firm on the wheel of the plow. It seems like little Esther is something Jeb never gets to. To be honest, Jeb resents her living each day. He stops his mind at the feeling. He just wants to get life back to normal. That's all. He's sorry though. He's filled with shame. He tells himself he should see each day with Esther as a blessing. When he gets to the hospital, he'll kiss the back of little Esther's head. He'll say it to God in his heart, he's sorry for the way he's carried on. But he'll speak up at the meeting with the doctors. He will not prolong her suffering. *It's time to let her go, Beth,* he'll say. *Medicine has done her no good. In heaven, she'll be healed.*

Jeb isn't long on the tractor, when Miriam comes from the back of the house toward the field. She looks pretty, every bit a young woman through the lifting haze of morning. She waves her arms. She fumbles over the ruts in the field. Jeb lifts the plow. He drives the tractor toward her. What does she want? Maybe she has a question about what to pack for her mother. Maybe unruly Zack and Job need a talking to. Perhaps, she's got word on the van. No, no. That's not it, Jeb thinks. She's come to tell him there's been a call from the hospital. *Could it be? Has God spared him from speaking his heart? Has it all been a test of faith? Has Miriam come with word that little Esther is gone?* At the thought, Jeb is sure; to lay Esther to rest is his most earnest desire.

Jeb is anxious to see Miriam's face up close, and from the distance, her expression is not clear. It seems like forever to get to her. He feels his eyes water, every bit of his heart longs to ask her, *Do you think I am a good father?* But he knows that Miriam would think it strange to hear such a thing. Certainly, she would respond just as Jeb would imagine. He'd jump from the tractor and embrace his sweet daughter, who he is so proud of, and kiss her on the head. She'd say, yes, he is a good father. But Miriam is not the one who Jeb needs to ask. It's none of the other children. Not even Beth. It's little Esther, whose voice he wants to hear. He'll want to see Esther first in heaven. He'll want to explain why he said no to another surgery. He tries to imagine that Esther has a voice to say it. Yet Jeb cannot hear Esther on earth, let alone in heaven, to tell him what he already knows. As Jeb nears Miriam, he swallows hard at the troubled look on her face. Then behind Miriam, in the distance, Jeb notices Pastor Fisher slowly walking around the house with his head down, holding his hat low at the waist.

GALLOWS' HILL

Sometime after one in the afternoon, Madison's mom was on the toilet with the door partly open. She told Madison she'd forgotten to mail out her car insurance. She needed to dodge the late fee and planned to pay it in person before the agency closed, if Madison wanted to tag along.

Madison didn't respond.

Her mom called through the house, feeling somewhere between what-the-hell and anger. She looked out into the yard, thinking, *There Madison goes taking off again*. She figured Madison left with her so-called group of friends from over at the Green Acres Trailer Court. A girl there named Alexa seemed to be the ringleader of the crew, always in the mix of some trouble.

"Do you think a real friend would lock you in a cubby?" Madison's mom asked her about a month ago. This was after Madison tore through the back door of their house heaving in tears. She stroked Madison's sweat-soaked hair, rolled the thick curls around her finger while Madison bawled into the sofa cushion. She wished gullible Madison had better senses. Lord knows, Madison, no different than any other fifteen-year-old, had a body running warp speed with a brain chugging along at a putter.

Madison was a husky girl and immature for her age. Madison still collected My *Little Pony,* Pokémon cards, and Happy Meal toys. In fact, Madison stroked a Barbie's hair and watched *Care Bear* repeats to sooth herself on the night of the cubby incident. Madison was pining for friends. She was caught giving them her jewelry. Even money. No surprise, a few days after her mom had it out with Alexa's kin over the cubby incident, Madison strutted in the door as though it were nothing. "Alexa explained the lock got stuck. And besides, she apologized," Madison told her mom.

"Think for once," Madison's mom responded that day, as Alexa flashed through her mind. She'd known Alexa since grade school. She'd worked on the line at the old cigar plant with Alexa's grandmother years ago, before it relocated to God-knows-where Mexico. And Alexa's grandma lived next door to Madison's aunt in the Green Acres. Madison's mom recalled, as a parent volunteer for the third grade Halloween party, how little Alexa yanked the pigtail of a girl who wouldn't give her candy. Then, Alexa had the nerve to console the girl. She even walked her to the teacher. Madison's mom cut Alexa off that day. "Be honest about what really happened," she said. Alexa stood with her finger to her mouth. She wouldn't fess up. She was sent to the timeout chair in the hall. Alexa went with a smile.

Well, it wasn't going to be Madison's head Alexa was yanking on now. Madison's mom would be sure of it. "Keep away from 'em. The whole lot of 'em," Madison's mom told her about Alexa and her crew. So, she was sure Madison had run off to meet them.

Madison's mom searched her bedroom. Madison was a stickler for order. It would be easy to see if anything was off. The shelves along the top of the wall were lined with collector Barbies. After playing with them, they all went back into the original boxes. *The Babysitters Club* series sat on top of the bookshelf for summer reading. Madison's mom had nagged her to get cracking on them. They sat barely touched. What stood out: Madison's backpack, covered with pins and badges, which she usually kept at the foot of the bookcase, was gone.

Madison's mom went back through the living room to fetch her keys off the old secretary. She expected to catch up with Madison down the road and give her an earful out the car window. When she reached the secretary though, she noticed the stubborn bottom drawer of it was out an inch or so. This was where she kept a tin safe with rainy day cash and her extra checkbooks. *No, surely not*, she thought as she kneeled on the floor. She gave the swollen drawer a tug, and it opened with a screech. By God, the money was gone. The checks too! Madison's mom called Madison's aunt at the Green Acres.

"If you see your niece roaming about the court, tell her, her a—is mine," she said.

Then she headed off in the car. She turned right onto the road, half a mile toward Green Acres. The road was on a hill in view of the old factories and mills by the river. Most were long shut up. The fading white *coal country* insignia painted across the tallest one, the old hardware factory at three stories high, showed like a ghost through the red brick. But not far down the road, there was no sign of Madison.

The girl had outsmarted her, likely taken the trails through the woods. Instead of driving the rest of the way to Green Acres, Madison's mom turned for home, just fuming. *Why run after the girl?* She'd leave Madison to the wolves. Let her come home on her own. But back at the house, she stewed over the theft. Then, she started to worry about her blank checks. They'd be in the hands of every junkie in the trailer court. Well, no kid of hers would be a thief. *I'll fix your hide,* Madison's mom thought. She dialed the police in her little town of Clearview, PA.

"I'd like to report a missing person," she said.

"Well, how long?" the voice on the other line asked.

Madison's mom had seen enough true crime shows to know about the 24-hour rule.

"Rather, I'd like to report a theft."

• • •

Around ten o'clock that same morning, Alexa awoke with fantasies of camping on a sandy Florida beach with her beau Jason. Just them and a fire under the stars. She put on her most comfortable sweat shorts. She'd be roughing it, holed-up in a car on the long drive to Florida for a few days before she'd set foot in the ocean.

Alexa zipped her bag. She took one last look around her bedroom. She'd actually miss the old, flowered bedding, the dingy wagon wheel wallpaper.

At the start of summer, Alexa's mom decided she'd stay long-term to care for her ailing grandma at Green Acres. "Maybe it will help you think of someone, for once, besides yourself," her mom told her. Sure, her grandma's place was a shut-up, wood-paneled trailer with a rust orange sofa, dingy shag carpet, and CBS, NBC, and PBS static on the rabbit ears. Yet it was still miles better than her mom's. Alexa and her mom were always butting heads. Besides, her mom had dumped Alexa off with her grandma as much as she could, all her life. She'd do anything to get Alexa, the oops baby, the reason she dropped out of high school, out of the way. When Alexa was five, her mom took up with her stepdad jerk-o, drunk-o Gary. He seemed to do no wrong in Alexa's mom's eyes. After Gary left welts on the back of Alexa's legs with a belt in the third grade, Alexa's mom said, "You get what you deserve." Then she had Alexa change from a skirt to pants for school. Then came Alexa's bratty-assed stepbrother and sister. Just a squeal when Alexa came near them, while they played with their toys, and Gary and her mom went apeshit on Alexa. So then, no wonder, Alexa would give them a good pinch or a whack when no one was looking and deny it. If she was going to get paddled regardless, she'd give them a real reason to fuss. On top of that, two wives and three kids after Alexa, her dad's place was no better than her mom's. Hence, her grandma's was the only place Alexa ever felt somewhat at home.

Her grandma was easygoing, but she was eighty. She used a walker and was incontinent. The woman's mind was slipping. Alexa would have to ask her, often at the smell, if she needed changing. Otherwise, her grandma would just sit in her dirty diaper without a word. Alexa would hold her breath to fight off a gag reflex through a diaper change. Her grandma's trailer smelled like sauerkraut and mothballs with shit and old-person stink on top of it. Alexa often went out the door on her way to school sniffing the inside of her shirt and spraying perfume, worried the odor lingered on her clothes.

Alexa closed her bedroom door. She tapped her fingers along the wall as she walked down the hall to her grandma's room to get her up for her morning bath.

Alexa helped her grandma out of bed, thinking how much she'd miss her. Alexa walked her to the bathroom and pulled off her wet diaper. She ran warm water, undressed her, and guided her into the bath. Alexa swiped the wet rag over the old woman's back. She shampooed her white hair. Her grandma sat, a pile of flub and wrinkles with saggy breasts that hung down her sides, quietly with her head trembling. The two used to talk more, but lately all Alexa's grandma ever said was, "Don't get old, sweetie." If Alexa ever shared anything about her life, she responded most often with, "Well, isn't that so."

After the bath, Alexa got her grandma into a fresh diaper and slipped a clean nightgown over her head. Alexa combed her hair. Alexa expected her mom and her two aunts would come to inspect the trailer, to be sure the weekly to-do list on the fridge they left for Alexa was all done. They might occasionally run the sweeper or wash some dishes, then watch game shows with the old woman. They'd act all high-and-mighty like they'd done the world for her. Perhaps, when Alexa was gone, they'd finally all realize just how much she did for her grandma.

By eleven o'clock, Alexa had her grandma in her lounge chair in the living room just in time for *The Price is Right*. She got her grandma's oatmeal and coffee and said, "Going to hang out with friends."

Her grandma didn't respond.

Alexa put on her boyfriend Jason's hoodie. She went onto her grandma's porch to wait for Jason and the others. She could smell Jason on the hood. Axe spray, Marlboros, and Tide. Alexa looked across the way, waiting for him to appear from the neighbor Tina's trailer, just catty-corner Alexa's grandma's.

Alexa recalled the first day she saw Jason, shortly after he came to Clearview, out smoking. She hadn't cared for smoking before this, but she stole a pack of cigarettes from the Uni-Mart next to Green Acres. She'd choke back a Marlboro menthol on her grandma's porch, nearly every time she spotted Jason out. She knew, one day, he'd be out and ask for a smoke. Just as planned, on a chilly, rainy day, Jason peered from under his black hoodie and called out, "Hey, can I bum a smoke?"

Alexa dashed through the downpour and hung out with Jason that day on Tina's porch. She took in every inch of him up-close with a deep drag of her cigarette. She wondered what he would think if he knew she'd already carved his name into her thigh with a paring knife. Jason told Alexa his mom was a junkie, originally from Clearview. She jumped around from state to state chasing the dragon. He said he'd even spent some time in foster care while his mom got clean, just for a while. Jason's mom was one of many burnouts coming and going at Tina's. Jason said his mom had a warrant in Florida for burglary. That was why she came back to Clearview. Not long after they arrived, though, Jason's mom was off to Sturgis, just for a week she claimed, with some biker she'd met at The Rambler bar in town. Three weeks had gone by since Jason had last heard from her.

"Man, I'd give anything to get back to Florida," Jason told Alexa. "I got a cousin I can crash with, if I can just find a way down."

"I've never been too far out of Clearview. I've always dreamed of seeing the beach," Alexa said.

"Ah, man," Jason said. "You'd love it. Let's go."

Finally, it was happening.

Alexa would steal a pack of smokes every few days from the Uni-Mart for her and Jason. He was always in awe outside the convenience store when Alexa pulled a stolen pack of Marlboros from the pouch of her oversized sweatshirt. Even better, Jason would keep watch while Alexa would schmooze some strung-out looking, forty-something guys, the types with names like Joe or Eddy with feathered hair in wife-beaters with jack-o'-lantern smiles. They'd buy her cartons and Big Bear forty ouncers, just for a bit of female attention. That is, until the Uni-Mart manager spotted Alexa stealing through the round security mirror above the door. The manager called the town cop on Alexa. Then the cop started parking in the lot. He'd step out of his cruiser just as Alexa would strut up to one of her goons.

But Alexa was one step ahead of the cop.

One day, Madison knocked on her door, the way she always did in the Acres looking for someone to hang out with. Instead of telling Madison she had to wash her grandma or get her supper, Alexa said, "I'll be right out. Just give me a minute." Then, she walked pathetic little childlike Madison over to the Uni-Mart, and from across the street, she said, "Madison, I have something very important for you to do. If you can pull it off, you can be in my club."

Madison's eyes widened like saucers.

Alexa realized that day, perhaps, Madison was her ticket out of town.

● ● ●

On the day she disappeared, Madison had actually taken a left on the road toward the trails that headed up to Gallows' Hill.

Her mom was nearly certain she was wearing a smiley face print T, since she couldn't find it in Madison's closet or in the dirty laundry. She was almost sure Madison had a pink scrunchie with her thick dark hair half pulled back. She was able to identify the badges on Madison's backpack with the help of Madison's aunt—ACDC, Slayer, a boom box, dice, praying hands, and a *hang in there* cat badge with a blue and pink lucky rabbit's foot.

Madison jogged down the road. Her backpack had three changes of clothes, toothpaste, deodorant, and tampons. It bumped clumsily against her sweaty back.

As Madison walked the berm of the winding road, a tan Chevette passed. The driver would call the police once Madison's missing person flyers went out. He'd report seeing a girl that sort of matched Madison's description there. He said, for sure, she was wearing a smiley face shirt. He would leave out that he was sifting through his CDs in the passenger seat of his car, that he saw Madison in the rearview mirror, stumbling out of the ditch, presumably, after he ran her off the berm.

Madison turned her head at the sound of the Chevette spitting gravel. Seeing that it didn't slow down or veer to avoid her, she retreated into the ditch. Because of this, her already worn Nikes were covered with mud. She returned to the road. She scraped her feet against the pavement. She cursed the driver as the water seeped into the soles of her shoes.

The afternoon sun was hot. Must have been in the eighties. Madison could feel the sweat bead down her bangs and the back of her neck. Once she reached the path in the woods, Madison fussed with her hair. She hated her thick, dark bob of wiry frizz. She pressed it tightly to her scalp into the scrunchie. She felt particularly self-conscious about her hair, especially since she'd be seeing Alexa. Alexa once said, in front of their crew, that Madison's hair looked like pubes. "Pubes?" Madison asked. "You know, the hair that grows between your legs," Alexa said with a laugh. Just the thought made Madison's cheeks swell with pins and needles. She could still envision Alexa, after pointing this out, running her fingers through her own fine hair. It wisped loosely back into place.

No qualms, Alexa could be a bully at times. At other times though, she was cool. Friends foremost, Madison reminded herself. *Besides, why else would Alexa invite her to run away with the crew?*

. . .

Madison's mom had a moment of regret after she hung up with the police. She reassured herself. It would be a hard lesson. Maybe a sit down with a cop might scare some sense into Madison. Then, a good talk with the family's pastor might make it right. Once Madison's father, a long-haul trucker, got to town at the end of the week, they'd figure out a punishment. Likely a grounding and a list of chores for Madison to work off the money she stole.

While she waited for the cop, she snooped around Madison's room. She thought there were some clothes missing, but she wasn't certain. Then, she tried to figure out how much money was in the tin safe. She sat at the kitchen table to recall how much she'd recently stashed in there and when. It had to be two hundred bucks or so, but she wasn't sure.

It was a quick visit with the town cop. He scratched a report on a yellow carbon copy pad with the date on the top, July 19, 1997. He handed the pad to Madison's mom to sign. The kids in Clearview referred to the cop as the town clown. Madison's mom hated to admit she found it funny. As she handed him back the pad, she recalled the day she passed him in her car. He stood in the little Veteran's Park in bubbles up to his knees. The teens had dumped a gallon of dish soap in the memorial fountain. Calling him in a time of crisis, she was plagued by the words *glorified babysitter* she used to describe him once at a town council meeting. She was one of the attendees in favor of cutting him from the budget.

The cop asked where Madison's mom thought Madison had gone off to with the money.

"Green Acres," Madison's mom said, before he even finished his sentence. "She has a crew she runs with there. Alexa's the one girl."

"Well, ma'am, I'll keep a lookout," the cop said, locking eyes with her for the first time.

She was quick to look away.

He handed her the carbon copy of the report.

She took it. She realized Madison would make the police log in the town paper.

"Kids," she said.

The man shrugged and nodded, it seemed, in agreement. "Call when she turns up," he said. "I'll come talk to 'er."

• • •

The crew—Kaylie, Cassidy, Tracey, Renee, Alexa, Jason, and Madison, talked about running away over the summer, during hangouts over stolen beers. The crew dangled their legs over the edge of the old coal tipple in the woods. The tipple was grown over with weeds and covered in graffiti, and the crew would drop the cans over the side and aim for targets on the rocks below.

Everyone in the crew had something to get away from. Kaylie's dad was just arraigned for statutory rape against one of her friends. Renee's mom liked swinging on her. Tracey was in charge of three young brothers. Her father was a vet who collected disability benefits for PTSD and spent most weeknights at The Rambler bar. Her mom got a bad knock in the head in a car wreck and lived in a stupor in front of the TV. For Alexa, the incident with Tina, the junkie neighbor, and Jason really made her want to get out of Clearview. Alexa noticed, for some time, the way slut-bag, cracked-out Tina looked at Jason with a gonna-getcha smile. Then, Tina said Jason owed her for staying on her dime. Tina told Jason she didn't need the little whore, referring to Alexa, laying around her place. One night, at nearly three a.m., Jason rapped at Alexa's bedroom window. Alexa peeked out, whispered "What's shaking?" She was shocked to find Jason in hysterics. "Imagine, waking up with that old thing, Tina, same age as your mom, on top of you. Rotten teeth and breath like a dragon. The fuck," he said. Then, Jason hunched in the grass in dry heaves. Alexa went outside. She crouched, wrapped her arms around Jason, and pulled his face into her. "Whatever it takes to get away from here, we'll do it," she promised.

Alexa sneaked Jason into her room that night. She coached Jason to hide under the bed if someone came in. She jumped at the slightest sound. On the odd occasion, Alexa's Aunt Denise came to crash at her grandma's trailer, after a hard night of drinking at The Rambler. She'd do this instead of driving the thirty minutes or so the rest of the way home in the cut. Alexa would catch hell if Denise caught a boy in her room. Worse, she'd tell Alexa's mom.

The situation with Tina and Jason pressed Alexa hard to go on the run. More than just talk.

Late that morning on July 19, she stood on her grandma's porch, relieved to see Tracey and Renee coming with their backpacks on.

"What a sicko," Tracey said, with her head turned to Tina's trailer, as she neared Alexa on the porch.

Alexa folded her arms, admiring Tracey, Renee, and her handiwork. They'd sprayed the word *PEDO* in red paint down the whole side of Tina's trailer. The letters rippled in the corrugated metal facade.

"Tina's fucking disgusting," Renee said.

"Glad we're getting the fuck out of this shit-hole town," Alexa said. "How much did you round up?" Alexa asked Tracey and Renee.

Tracey and Renee unbundled wads of cash, and the three girls counted it. However, between them, there was less than a hundred dollars. Alexa regretted she hadn't cleared her grandmother's bank account before her mom and aunts got hold of her social security benefits. Then, the fear of getting caught came over her. She imagined her mom and two aunts kicking her into the dirt of her grandma's lot.

"Let's hope Madison comes through," Alexa said.

She thought back on the day Madison, the snitch, moseyed by her porch and asked, "What's doing?"

"Up for stealing some smokes?" Alexa asked Madison that day. I need something more," Alexa said. "Can you keep a secret?"

"Yeah," Madison said and nodded that day.

We're all running away to Florida, for real. You too. Top secret. But we need money. Any way you can— Look, we'll talk more about it when you come back with smokes."

Back on the porch, on July 19, Tracey tied her shoe. Renee held her long, dark hair in front of her glasses, complaining about her split ends. Jason came out of Tina's door with his backpack on. He looked sharply at Alexa and flipped up his black hoodie.

When he stepped onto the porch, Alexa imagined he'd grab her and pull her in close for a kiss. Instead, Jason said hey and gave a slight wave. Then, Jason pulled out a pack of smokes and handed one to Alexa.

"Where's mine?" Tracey asked.

Jason looked up, exhaled, and slid a cigarette out of the package. He held it up to Tracey. She snatched up the cigarette. Then, Jason pulled out his lighter. He lit Alexa's cigarette first. Alexa felt that familiar quiver of attraction in her chest. She caught the lozenge and smoke of Jason's mouth.

Jason was Alexa's first. They'd haul up in his room at Tina's on a futon. Alexa remembered the day Jason got keyed up watching *Two Thousand Maniacs,* some old horror movie from the seventies he had on a VCR tape. Jason pulled Alexa into him. He reached into her shorts. He unbuckled his belt and unzipped his jeans. The macabre organ music and the scream of women played on the television. It was a few minutes of sex. After, Jason didn't cradle Alexa in his arms. He didn't gaze into her eyes, as she'd imagined. Rather, he zipped his pants quickly and fastened his belt. He rolled back across the futon on the opposite side of Alexa. He gave her a nudge with his foot, like something someone might do to a kid. *That was it?* Alexa questioned. Jason rewound the flick. "Watch this," he said with a smile. In the film, a man was getting a lady to touch a knife. Then, he cut her finger nearly off.

Alexa realized early on that Jason loved gory films: *Texas Chainsaw, Last House on the Left, Cannibal Holocaust.* He'd watched the *Maniacs* movie repeatedly. In spite of the sex, Alexa memorized nearly every bit of the *Maniacs* script. The movie was about a Confederate, Civil War-era ghost town. The town's people invited Yanks down for a centennial celebration. They tortured the Yanks, of course. Dismembered a lady named Bea. Quarter-drew a man named John with horses. Rolled a character named David down a hill in a barrel of spikes.

"Yoo-hoo," Tracey said, waving her hand in front of Alexa's face. "The money situation."

"How much we got?" Jason asked.

"Let's hope Madison comes through or we won't get much further than the Pizza Station," Alexa said.

"What about the hunting camps at Meese Crossroads? Most are empty. It's not far from Gallows' Hill, and we have a day to kill," Renee said. "Might lift some shit that we can pawn."

Jason nodded and pointed to Renee. "Genius," he said.

"Why not?" Alexa asked.

Alexa took a drag.

"Here's to a day of smashing windows and kicking in doors," Tracey said.

• • •

Seemed in Clearview, if things didn't happen on the school ballfield or in a church basement, there was hardly a thing to do. Madison's mom could count on one hand the kids that frequented either place. More often, skateboarders did tricks on the sidewalks. Cruisers raced in their cars down Front Street. Their glass-pack mufflers let out a deafening roar. The stoners loafed in the Veteran's Park across from the Pizza Station and sat on the tops of the benches in clouds of smoke. All the cliques would ban together for a party in the woods. While the other storefronts were run-down, empty on the street, as night closed in, The Pizza Station's bright neon sign illuminated a near-carnival atmosphere of teens. The trash bin next to the front door spilled out onto the walk.

There was no word on Madison at the Green Acres, when her mom called her aunt for the third time that day.

Madison's mom drove to the bank in person to put a hold on her account. The Pizza Station was close by, so she walked over, thinking it might be just the place to find Madison. A little after five o'clock, she stormed across the street. The concrete was dotted with snuff spit, ciga-rette butts, and the glossy, brown spots of chewed-up gum. She stepped over a greasy tissue paper of priced-by-the-slice pizza and a gnawed-up crust. She flung open the glass storefront door. A shopkeeper's bell rang overhead.

Madison's mom couldn't get over the glassy-eyed teens. They loafed at the tables with their hoodies up. Shame, she thought, none of their parents likely cared where they were as long as they were out of the house. Outside the new 24-hour Wal-Mart off the interstate, where Madison's mom worked as a cashier, The Pizza Station was the only place still open in town past nine. All the volunteers on Clearview's town council said, "If we only had the revenue for a YMCA." Madison's mom researched grants and donors, but there was no way they could swing such a place in Clearview.

Madison's mom went from table to table asking if any of the teens there had seen Madison. They all said no. A group said they didn't even know her, so Madison's mom pulled her most recent school photo from the billfold in her purse and held it out over their table. The teens sunk quietly in their seats, shaking their heads no. They side-eyed and smirked at one another. This made Madison's mom feel like she had two heads. Yet she was still the only person who made sense in the world.

• • •

It was about a mile walk down the old railroad bed through the forest to Gallows' Hill. This is where Alexa told Madison the gang would meet. The Clearview townies exaggerated witch trials and a mass lynching at the hill, but Madison discovered, as a report topic for school, that there was only one hanging there, ever. Some horse thief that shot a farmer in the late eighteen hundreds.

Once she settled her hair, Madison reached into her pocket to be sure the two hundred dollars was still there. She rolled it in her fingers and pushed it deep in her pocket. Madison imagined her mom's nagging voice. Just the same as the sound of her shoes crunching along the shell of the path. The voice warned her about walking alone. It talked up the dangers of the woods. Warned of the old, abandoned mineshafts dotting the trail. Madison passed one, cut into the hill, posted with a danger sign. "Who the fuck would even go near there?" Madison argued aloud to her mom, as though she were there. Then, she recalled her mom saying, "Keep away from 'em. The whole lot of 'em." Madison huffed at the thought of her mom trying to come between her and her friends. Then, Madison recalled how her mom even once told her that the occult met in the woods, on the prowl for a virgin sacrifice. Her mom held the newspaper in front of her face. It had a photo of a pentagram that had been turfed by quads in the dirt of a strip mine clearing next to the woods. "Bullshit, Ma," Madison snapped back. "The Winters boys did that to scare everyone in town." The racing thoughts were enough to make Madison stop in her tracks for a few seconds, shake her head, and roll her shoulders to gather herself.

Madison wouldn't miss her mom's nagging. In fact, Madison's only regret was that she'd miss *Saturday Evening Gore Fest* on cable, and this week, they were playing one of her favorite horror movies, *Two Thousand Maniacs.* She'd seen the movie twice already. She'd watched it with her face close to the screen and the volume low. She always had to be ready to flick the channel. Her Jesus-freak mom would pop her head in Madison's room willy-nilly. She'd have a cow about that type of filth in her house. No more, Madison thought. By evening, she'd be free down the highway under the night sky, on her way to a new life in Florida with her friends.

Madison took a deep breath. She could hear the others at the top of Gallows' Hill. She pulled her shirt from a V of sweat over her breasts. She swiped back the frizz of her hair with the sweat from her forehead. She ran her fingers through the waistband of her jean shorts. She'd cut her food portions in half over the past few weeks. She was down ten pounds, and the fabric rippled beneath her belt, which was fastened two more loops tighter than before. Madison stretched through her back, preparing for the incline of Gallows' Hill. She moved her hands to the top of her hips, felt her 5'2", 170-pound body all the way through. She quickly forgot any sign of the loss.

Madison stepped up over the ruts and twisted roots to the top of the hill.

She could hear Jason clearly as she neared the top.

"You can get some money for these," he said.

Madison took a heavy step to crest the hill. Her knee buckled against her chest.

Madison locked eyes on Jason first. He was on the other side of the fire pit lined with stones and littered with beer cans. He squatted low to the ground with his elbows resting on his knee. He looked over a hoard of things strewn about the ground. An empty laundry satchel laid at his side. He had a couple of hunting knives. Brass knuckles. A new tarp folded in plastic. Boxes of shells. A couple of liquor bottles, all less than half full. A long, heavy rope.

Jason was lanky, fair-haired, and fair-skinned. He had on a black Metallica shirt. Though it was terribly hot, he wore jeans. A wallet chain hung from his waist.

Madison perked out her chest as she looked him over, but quickly sunk it back in when Jason looked up at her.

He didn't say hi. Just dropped his head back to the things on the ground.

Madison slipped her backpack from her arms and sat it with the others on the ground near a log used for a bench. Her eyes washed over the crew through the glare of the late-day sun. It shined like a bright spot and beamed through the branches of the treetops. Madison saw Alexa, across the fire pit, talking with Renee and Tracey. Kaylie and her boyfriend Cassidy sat on the log near the bags. Madison sized Alexa up, trying not to look obvious. It had been two weeks since Madison had last seen Alexa. Her hair was dyed bottle-blond. She looked girly. Not the tomboy Madison always knew her to be. Alexa had a beer in one hand, a cigarette in the other.

Alexa glanced at Madison, without breaking from her conversation. When their eyes met, Madison, in those few seconds, felt the sting of how badly Alexa had made her feel over the cubby incident: The gang was drinking beers at crackhead Tina's trailer. Alexa suggested they play the make-out game seven minutes in heaven. Madison went into the cubby, hoping for Jason to come inside its door. However, she waited for what seemed like eternity. No one came. When she finally pushed on the door, it was locked from the outside. Surely, by Alexa. Madison begged and banged on the door for what must have been thirty minutes or so. She couldn't recall any commotion at the door, any consolation from her friends. She kicked the door open. The crew was gone. Madison ran off in tears—

Let bygones be bygones, she told herself, as she stood tall on the hill.

• • •

Alexa acted as though she hadn't noticed Madison. But she couldn't shake what resurfaced every time she set eyes on her. When the two were around eleven, they played in the yard outside of Madison's aunt's trailer. Sure, when they were kids, Alexa played with Madison, but it was more for the Hi-C juice boxes, the Fruit Wrinkles and Roll-Ups, the Go-Gurt and snack packs of Sour Patch Kids on hand at Madison's aunt's. It was all the stuff in the store Alexa's mom had her put back on the shelves. Instead, she got the Little Hug Juicies, ten for three dollars that came in the weird plastic barrel-shaped containers with the foil lids that never peeled right off the edges. Sure, it was a long time ago, but Alexa still recalled how Madison fussed over her Barbie's skirt when it got a speck of dirt on it. Alexa sipped on her Kool-Aid drink pouch while she ogled Mr. Tucker next door while he worked on his old Ford pickup. His muscular arms dimpled as he moved them under the sun-faded green hood. He spit chewing tobacco on the ground. He was covered in monkey grease. It made Alexa tingly inside. She tied the front of her shirt in a knot, strutted over, and leaned against the fender of Mr. Tucker's truck. "Wha-cha fixin'?" Alexa asked. She told him she was bored, playing dolls—ya' know, kids' stuff, as she beamed up at him. Mr. Tucker lifted his head from under the hood. He wiped his big hands on a grease rag, while looking down on Alexa. She wondered if he noticed *that longing* as she swallowed down the lump in her throat waiting for him to look around, see that no one was watching, and ask her to go inside. But no, Mr. Tucker said, "The engine block. Now you best run along. There's heavy stuff here, and I don't want you to get hurt." Then he put his hand on the top of Alexa's head and nudged her away from the fender. Alexa sank inside as she walked back across the lawn, just as Madison started to ask, "You want to play some more?" But Alexa told her, "No. I'm sick of all your little kid stuff." For years, Alexa didn't want anything to do with Madison, until she could get her to steal smokes.

Meanwhile, Madison fanned the front of her smiley face T for air, as she looked over the group at the top of Gallows's Hill.

"Hey girlie," Madison heard Kaylie say.

"Hey," Cassidy said while clearing his throat.

Madison noticed his glossy, stoner eyes.

"Hey," Madison responded. She hunched over and unzipped her bag. "What's with all the stuff Jason has? I thought we were barebones."

Kaylie leaned her head into Madison and flipped her hair over her left shoulder.

"So, Jason, Alexa, Renee, and Tracey broke into some hunting camps. Shit to pawn for the trip, I guess," Kaylie said quietly. Then, Kaylie coughed and flipped her head back around.

Madison slipped her hand into her backpack, feeling deep into the center of the fabric. She heard Tracey talking to Alexa and Renee. Tracey was always loud and braggy. The brute who ruled the hallways on the odd day she came to school. Heaven forbid Tracey find out, but behind her back, Madison referred to her as Sasquatch.

"So I said bitch step-up and pop-off. So the bitch swung, and I laid her out in one hit," Tracey said. She punched her arm through the air.

"Oh my God, she did too," Renee said. "I thought the bitch was dead."

Alexa laughed.

"Bitches get what they deserve," Tracey said. She took a gulp of her beer.

"Stupid fucking cunt," Alexa said and took a chug of her beer.

Madison looked down, not to be accused of eavesdropping. She pulled the checkbook from the backpack. She stood up and stepped over to Jason, who was still looking over his things. Madison held the checkbook over Jason's head.

Jason looked up. He snatched it from her hand and flipped through the empty pages.

"Cool. Where's the money?" Jason asked.

Madison reached deep into her right pocket. She pulled out the crumpled, damp wad of cash.

Jason stood. He tucked the checkbook into his back pocket. He took the bills and started to unfold them. His hands were at Madison's eye level.

"It's two hundred," she said.

"Beer's behind me in the cooler," Jason replied. He wiped his jaw on his left shoulder, his eyes set on the bills.

Madison's arm brushed around Jason as she looked for the cooler. She spotted the bright pink cooler behind a nearby elm tree, and she went over there. She opened the lid and swiped her arm through a sea of melting ice to grab one of the five or so cans floating at the surface. She popped the tab. She walked back to Kaylie and Cassidy.

"So, I heard Jason tell Alexa, the dude they found to hitch a ride with said he might not have room for everybody," Kaylie said. Her left hand cradled her neck.

Madison thought, *Well that's just fucked up.* Her lips tightened. She took a heavy breath through her nose. She expected she'd be the first one cut out of the trip. She swallowed down the lump, huffed through the sting in her cheeks. It felt like a cannonball dropped in her stomach.

The pressure inside Madison had burst like a balloon.

"When the fuck are we leaving?" Madison asked.

The gang shot glances at one another.

"Okaaaay," Alexa said.

Then, Alexa, Tracey, and Renee laughed and rolled their eyes.

Kaylie and Cassidy stayed quiet. They kept their elbows on their knees. They looked to the ground with their faces in their hands.

Jason grinned ear-to-ear. He clapped loudly. "You're bad-ass, Madison," Jason scoffed.

"Really, Jason, when are we leaving?" Madison repeated.

"Look, I'm trying to work it out. The guy said he probably doesn't have room for everyone, but it's no big deal. He travels back and forth every month or so. He can take some of you the next time he comes through town," Jason responded.

Madison folded her arms and planted her feet firm on the ground.

"Look, just chill the fuck out. Whoever can go will go," Jason said.

"Well, I didn't give you two hundred dollars for a fucking beer. If I don't go, I want it back. I swear, Jason, if I'm stuck here, I'll tell everyone where you've all gone off to."

Alexa spit out her drink.

Renee asked, "Did you just hear what she fucking said?"

Alexa, Tracey, and Renee closed back into each other.

"Fucking snitch," Alexa said.

Madison planted her face into her beer can and gave it a shake. It was almost empty. She finished it off, then tossed it into the fire pit.

"You know what," Tracey said. "Here's to getting the fuck out of here, away from snitchy bitches." She raised her beer to Renee and Alexa.

Jason scooped up a bottle of whiskey from the ground. He took off the cap, tossed it into the pit, and lifted the bottle in the air.

"I propose a loyalty shot. To the runaway gang," Jason said. He tipped the bottle to his mouth and leaned back with a big gulp.

"To the runaway gang," Alexa, Tracey, and Renee cheered.

Jason finished the shot. Then, he held the bottle out to Madison, shaking it a bit.

"Drink it. Drink it," Tracey and Renee chanted.

"Yeah, drink it," Jason said, squinting with a pinch in his throat.

Alexa stepped forward and said, "Everyone who plans on leaving with us is taking a shot."

Madison turned to Kaylie and Cassidy, seeking some assurance. However, Cassidy lit a cigarette that rested loosely in his mouth. Kaylie nervously shook her crossed legs.

Madison took the bottle from Jason's hand.

"Ten count," Alexa said.

Madison stared down the lip of the bottle. Then she brought the whiskey to her mouth. Beer was one thing, but whiskey! The smell choked her right away, and she stifled her breath before it touched her lips. It was all she could do to keep from turning her head to gag.

Madison flipped her head back to the count of the group: One thousand one. One thousand two—

The count felt like eternity, and when Madison heard ten, she pulled away from the bottle. She squinted sharply. She yanked her shirt up over her mouth and gagged into it. She brushed her tongue against the fabric to rid herself of the taste.

She could hear Tracey say, ever so faintly, "Choke on it, snitch."

Renee coughed, "Snitch."

"Kaylie's next," Alexa said.

Madison took the insults all in with the gulp. She felt she deserved the slack for running off crying to her mom. With her face still planted in her shirt, she passed the bottle to Kaylie. Then she leaned forward with her hands on her knees. She heard Kaylie say, "You guys are fucking retarded."

"Kaylie! Don't say that word in front of Madison," Alexa said.

Madison pulled her shirt away from her mouth.

"Get bent," Madison told Alexa.

Kaylie, still firmly seated on the log, was finishing off her ten-count. At ten, Kaylie parted the whiskey bottle from her lips and raised her right, middle finger into the air.

Cassidy finished off his shot next. Then, Tracey. Then, Renee. Then, it was Alexa's turn.

"She has to count to twenty," Jason jeered.

Alexa lifted the bottle to her mouth.

"Fuck off, Jason," Alexa said. Then she tipped the whiskey back.

Madison felt nauseous and hot. The alcohol seemed to slow everything down. Her nerves got the best of her. *What if she couldn't go? How would she get the money and the checkbook back? Had her mom already discovered them missing? Would her mom be waiting for her with the police when Madison got home?* Madison envisioned her mom with her arms folded and a stern face waiting at the door. All this flooded Madison amidst a barrage of insults. Tracey, Renee, and Alexa spewed words like pussy, bitch, cunt and more coughs to the sound of snitch. Madison wasn't sure if they were all meant for her or aimed at everyone in the group.

Madison's face sunk to the ground. She felt a warm hand on her back. She heard a voice. It was Kaylie asking, "Madison, you okay?"

"She's fine," Madison heard Alexa say.

"Take a drink," Kaylie said. She handed Madison water in a plastic bottle. The half-empty bottle crinkled when she took a big gulp. She parted the bottle from her lips. She noticed Jason had fashioned a slip-knot into a rope from his hoard. He tossed the lasso toward Tracey, Renee, and Alexa.

Jason laughed out, "Almost got you that time."

The lasso landed and slid from the side of Alexa's head.

"Jason!" Alexa said. Then, she turned sharply back to Renee and Tracey.

Jason kept tossing the lasso. He moved closer to Alexa, until after several tries, he snagged Alexa over the shoulders and drew the lasso tight. He slowly pulled her toward him. He gave Alexa a kiss on the cheek from behind her. Then, Alexa peeled the rope over her head.

Then, Jason tossed the rope onto a branch of the elm tree in front of the cooler. After a few tries, it fell over the branch. The slipknot fashioned as a lasso moments ago, now, swayed as a hangman's noose.

"OK, guys, listen up," Jason said with the hangman's end of the noose wrapped in his left hand. "There's a reason why we're starting our journey at Gallows' Hill. If we're going to beg, borrow, steal, even kill if we have to, to get the fuck out of this town, we need to know who's loyal. Everyone is going to put their neck into the noose and pledge loyalty to the runaway gang."

The group fell silent.

Alexa seized the noose and placed her head into the center.

"Do you pledge loyalty to the gang? Never to snitch, even if we have to steal or kill?" Jason asked.

"I do," Alexa said.

Jason drew his arms into his ribs, adding tension.

Alexa remained silent, looking to the ground. She'd expected a gentle tug from Jason, but instead, he plied pressure on the noose. It knocked her off balance, and she changed her footing to counter the pull. The rough burlap rope scratched against her neck.

Jason loosened the noose.

Alexa lifted the rope from her head.

"This is fucked," Kaylie said looking up at Alexa.

"I'll go next," Jason said. He held the end of the rope to Renee.

Renee took hold of it as Jason put his head in the noose.

Renee pulled lightly. The rope remained slack.

"You have to pull harder, since he's tall," Tracey said.

Alexa stepped behind Renee. They both leaned back on the noose. It tightened on Jason's neck.

"Oh my God, this feels so weird," Jason said with a smile, as the rope closed in.

"Do you pledge loyalty to the runaway gang, to never snitch?" Renee asked.

"No," Jason said. Then he laughed.

Renee and Alexa leaned further back into the rope.

"Fucking asshole," Tracey said through a smile.

"Even if we have to steal or kill?" Alexa asked. She let go of the rope and stepped to Jason. She poked her finger into his ribs.

"I do," Jason said. His voice took on a serious tone.

Jason pulled the noose off of his neck with his hands and stepped out of it.

Renee passed the end of the rope to Tracey.

Renee put her head in the noose.

Tracey pulled the rope around Renee's throat.

Jason offered up the pledge.

"I do," Renee said.

Tracey pulled the rope with both arms. Her elbows came flush to her sides as she pulled down on the rope.

"Are you sure?" Alexa asked. Alexa stepped directly in front of Renee and looked into her eyes. She always thought Renee was a flake, someone who'd go along with whomever she was around. She recalled how Renee never said boo to her in the halls at school when she was with her art club peeps. She recalled how Renee laughed and chatted with the stoners in gym class while she changed in the adjacent stall by herself. If something went down, Alexa was sure, Renee would turn on the crew.

Madison got goosebumps as she watched Renee in the noose. A chill rolled through her spine as Alexa snapped to Tracey, "Tighter!"

"Yes. Yes. Yes," Renee said.

"Absolute?" Alexa asked.

Renee's eyes teared. She lifted her hands about her neck and pried her fingers between her throat and the noose.

"No way," Alexa scolded Renee. "Hands back down. One more time."

Alexa repeated the loyalty pledge.

Renee fought her elbows down and made a choking sound. Again, she said, "Yes."

"Just stop. Stop," Kaylie protested from across the pit. "You're hurting her."

Jason lifted his finger to his mouth, shushing Kaylie.

Tracey leaned further back on the rope.

Renee's feet lifted to the tips of her toes.

Madison put her hand to her own neck. She anticipated the tug of the noose closing in tightly around her own throat. She started to cry and tremble. But she was determined. She couldn't go back home. If it was allegiance that the crew wanted, that's what she'd give.

Tracey loosened the rope, and Renee fell to her knees.

Alexa and Jason released the noose and lifted Renee.

Renee gripped her neck with her left hand.

"Next up," Tracey said, waving on Cassidy.

"Let her know how it feels," Kaylie spoke through her teeth, as Cassidy stepped away from Kaylie's side to the hangman's end of the noose.

Tracey put her head through the noose, as Cassidy tightened it firm and spoke the loyalty pledge.

Tracey said, "I do."

Cassidy leapt up from the ground. A gasp expelled from the group at the prospect of Cassidy's full weight touching back down. It would surely have done Tracey in. However, Cassidy released the rope mid-air before coming to the ground. He stumbled forward as the end of the rope whipped freely in the air. There was a burst of laughter among the group as Tracey turned, her head still in the noose. She grabbed Cassidy's collar and slapped him over the head. "Faggot bitch," she said.

Madison did not laugh like the others. The thoughts of her turn on the noose played far too heavy. She'd prove she wasn't a snitch and just as capable as the others to steal, kill, do whatever it took to get the hell out of town. *What did she have to lose by slipping the noose on her neck?* Maybe it was something she deserved, after all. She'd stolen from her mom, and for what? Ah yes, she remembered, a crack at freedom, the wind whipping through her hair on the open road to God-knows-where, making it on her own. She'd prove it to the world. She imagined calling her mom, briefly from a payphone. She'd refuse to disclose her location. Just let her know she was alive—that's all—and making it without her.

When the group resettled, Cassidy took his place in the noose.

Kaylie positioned herself at the hangman's end.

"You better pull that shit too. Little fucker," Tracey heckled them.

Kaylie pulled the noose snug to Cassidy's neck. He said the pledge. The rope was loosened.

Then, Kaylie placed the noose around her neck.

"Come on, Madison. It's your turn to pull the noose," Jason said.

He looked at Madison sharply.

"Madison. Come on," she heard the others shout.

Madison couldn't budge. She couldn't muster a response.

Jason stepped over to Madison. He shook her by the shoulders.

"I can't. I just can't," Madison said.

"Fucking baby," Alexa said.

Alexa then stepped into the hangman's position.

Kaylie's eyes widened as Alexa took the rope.

Cassidy jutted forward, with his chest out and his arms open ready to swoop in at any moment.

"Do you pledge loyalty to the runaway gang? To never snitch, even if we must steal and kill?" Alexa asked.

"I do," Kaylie said.

Alexa tilted back with the rope.

Kaylie's heels lifted from the ground.

Cassidy leaned over Alexa. He pulled upward on the rope, countering Alexa's weight.

"OK. Enough," Cassidy said. He nudged Alexa out of the way with his hip. The rope slackened, and Kaylie touched flat, back on the ground.

Kaylie burst into tears.

Alexa snapped her head and rolled her eyes as Cassidy assisted Kaylie in loosening the noose from her neck. Kaylie rubbed her neck. Cassidy ushered her away from the noose.

"No way. No way," Kaylie yelled back at Alexa as she walked away. "Fuck you all. You're all psycho. No way am I going anywhere with you."

Kaylie grabbed her backpack. Then Cassidy, at Kaylie's heels, grabbed his.

Alexa and Tracey barked, "Yeah that's right, bitch. Go, you fucking baby. You never had it in ya'. Go back home to your fucking pervert daddy."

"Fuck off," Cassidy yelled back. Cassidy and Kaylie disappeared on the trail from Gallows' Hill.

"Well, that clears up two seats," Renee said.

"OK, Madison. You're next," Alexa said.

Madison stood tall with a gulp. She walked over to the noose and slipped it around her neck.

"That's right! Yeah! Fuck yeah," Renee and Tracey cheered. It was just what Madison longed for. She'd show them she wasn't the girl anymore who freaked in the closet. She was nothing to mess with and matched them, every last one of them. Hell-or-high-water, she was going on the run.

"Let her say the pledge," Jason said.

"Fuck the pledge. We already know she's a snitch," Alexa jeered.

• • •

Forty-eight hours after the crew ran off, their mothers hung flyers around Clearview. They banged on every door in the Acres. Then, they met up at Alexa's grandma's trailer to watch the first missing person's reports on the news. The TV was on in advance of the six o'clock news and could be heard outside. Alexa's grandmother stood on her porch, hunched over her walker. Her head trembled and she made a mumbling sound. Madison's aunt rested her back against the outside of the porch rail. She smoked and looked up through the wisps of her permed hair into the bright blue sky. Alexa's mom kicked the dirt, her head down with her arms folded over her breast. Madison's mom wiped the sweat from her nape below her frizz of pinned-up hair.

The last time Madison's mom had seen Alexa's was in her checkout line at Wal-Mart. Alexa's mom had asked how she lucked on at the new 24-hour Super Center. "It was like winning the lottery," Madison's mom told her as she rang the woman's Jiffy peanut butter and eighty-nine cent loaf of bread. Really, though, it was because she'd long befriended one of the shift managers who also volunteered on the town council. "You know how many applications they got? Must have been three thousand for a hundred positions," she told Alexa's mom. Alexa's mom turned her head through a crick in the neck. "If ever I can, I'll put in a word. I'm just a peon, but you never know," Madison's mom said, just to ease a world of disappointment on the tired woman's face. Alexa's mom reached deep into her purse to round up change. Seeing her again, she felt bad she never did put in a word to the manager, and all her thoughts on telling the woman off, that she ought to put her kid on a leash, escaped her fast. Besides, it seemed she'd raised a brat of her own. The two knuckleheads and their friends let loose in the world was a terrifying thought. And with that boy Jason, at that. Madison's mom didn't even know about him until they all ran off. Tina had tipped them off about the boy's goofball plan to run off to Florida. "Messing with fifteen-year-old girls," Tina said, pointing to the word *PEDO* sprayed on her trailer, going on about how the boy stirred up all kinds of trouble.

Now the women tried to piece the details of their daughters' last moments at home. They talked about what was missing from their homes and the times each girl left the house. When the six o'clock news came on, the women ran inside. They crowded around the sofa, as the pictures and descriptions of the crew flashed on the news. Madison's mom prayed her kid had enough sense to, at least, call home to say they were all OK.

"Something's got to be done with Alexa. Maybe a detention center or something," her mom said when Alexa appeared on the screen.

Just the thought of Madison left to fend for herself in a place like that! Her mom hadn't thought that far ahead to the consequences of the theft. Then the very public running away. Her little Madison was in for a world of trouble when she returned home.

As the women watched the news, the gang was well on the road to Florida. Alexa was the one who finagled the ride with one of her Joes, who was often headed South for reasons unknown. Alexa had originally planned to ditch the gang. She originally told Joe she'd show up alone and expected to schmooze him to take Jason along. She planned to play up that she and Jason were just friends, that she was helping the kid out of a bad situation. Jason was prepared to stand nearby while Alexa flirted their way into Joe's car. If that didn't work, Jason planned to ambush the guy with a knife. So, imagine Joe's surprise when Alexa showed up with all the others. Alexa cradled her chest in her arms and leaned into the passenger window of Joe's dinged-up Chevy Cavalier. She begged him to take the others along. They piled into the back before he could decide on his own. Somewhere outside of Atlanta, Alexa rested her head against the window of the passenger seat. She looked out through her reflection, dreading *the Joe's* hand as it crept toward her leg from the gearshift. She took shallow breaths with all the wet dog, but people, odor of the crew in the cab.

Alexa was already scripting in her mind what she'd say about Madison at the idea of being caught. She'd say the tug at the noose was meant to be just a good scare. She'd say the other's pressured her, and she was afraid for her own life if she didn't do as she was told. Really, Jason, Renee, and

Tracey were just as much to blame. *Why would she do such a horrific thing?*
If Alexa was really honest with herself, though the words would never
come out of her mouth, it had a lot to do with the day the two girls were
eleven, the day Madison witnessed Alexa's humiliation with Mr. Tucker.
Sure, the image of Madison on the noose reeled through Alexa's mind.
However, if it truly troubled Alexa, she'd never let it show. Instead, *Served
Madison right,* she more often thought. Any one of the crew could have
hung that day, just the same, including her.

So what was that final moment like for Madison? When Madison stood
under the noose at Gallows' Hill with her eyes wide shut, she managed to
get her hands up to her neck. However, the noose was too tight, tighten-
ing more by the second. Madison's fingers fumbled with panic when she
could not get them between the noose and her throat. Alexa buckled her
knees into her chest, swinging on the rope with all of her weight.

In the final moment, on July 19, 1997, Madison longed for her
mom's voice as she slipped out of consciousness. She came down hard
to the ground deep into herself. As she lay flat on her back, as though
asleep, she opened her eyes once, thinking perhaps she'd just passed out.
She heard her own death gurgle as though it were far off in the distance.
She caught the sun through the treetops one last time. She saw Alexa step
into the visage of the rolling branches above her. Alexa's fine hair danced
in wisps with the subtle breeze. She held a rock from the fire pit. Alexa
dropped it down on Madison. Quietly, Madison was gone.

Jason, Renee, Tracey, and Alexa pulled Madison's body through the
dirt to the edge of the hill and rolled her over the side. Her body snagged
on a fallen tree trunk, still in sight from the top of Gallows' Hill. Jason
skidded after Madison's corpse and yanked it further down by the leg
into a ravine some fifty feet below. He covered Madison with brush and
yelled for assurance from the others that Madison's corpse was concealed.

Madison's mom would get the call nearly a week later to come to the
police station. The talk from the police. It would take her time to make
sense of it, something about the woods. "Outside of Atlanta?" she'd ask.
"You mean, you found them hauled out in the woods? Florida?"

"No, no," they'd say. "Just Madison." Repeat, "Madison's body, covered in brush in Clearview, just off of Gallows' Hill."

The round of cheers from the kids at The Pizza Station at the first news reports of hometown kids, like Bonnie and Clyde, fell hush at the report of Madison's murder. The media portrayed the runaway gang as misfits and Clearview as a go-nowhere, inbred, rust-belt town. A place so far turned in itself its teens were capable of torturing and hanging a simple-minded girl. The teens at The Pizza Station who looked puzzled, unfamiliar with Madison's name or face the day her mom came table to table to find her . . . They'd all harbor memories of it with deep regret for the rest of their lives, certain of Madison's face on the news, certain that their paths had crossed.

After Madison's body was discovered, her mom scurried past loafing customers at the Wal-Mart. They talked about the murder in the aisles. She regretted she lived in a town small enough to know what happened, but big enough to not realize she was that hanged girl's mom. Day in and day out she'd rush her cash drawer to her register to avoid all the murmur of Madison's murder. She'd recall the dredge of her own feet on the footpath to Gallows' Hill from when she went to see for herself, the spot where her daughter died.

Worse, Madison's mom would fold her hands in her Wal-Mart smock, flick off her check-out light, and make a dash for the breakroom in tears at the sight of Alexa's mom in the check-out line a few registers down. Sure, she fantasized about running up to her, beating at her chest, screaming. There were times she still looked at the door expecting Madison to strut in the house. But then she figured, what good would making such a scene do? The closed-casket funeral of a hanging victim with her face smashed in by a rock, left in the woods, was no proper goodbye after all. But never another word was spoken between the two women after Madison's body was recovered, after Alexa was tried as an adult and sentenced to life. Besides, Alexa's mom had nowhere else in Clearview to shop. For the two women, every sighting relived Clearview's newest legend, the hanging at Gallows' Hill. They avoided one another, same as folks in Clearview knew to avoid the abandoned mineshafts all around the town.

ABOUT THE AUTHOR

MICHAEL LOCKETT has a B.A. in Communication from Clarion University and an MFA in Creative Writing from Carlow University. He's a lover of the short story and inspired by the works of Breece D'J Pancake, Lewis Nordan, and Catherin Mansfield. His stories are published in the Northern Appalachian Review, Prometheus Dreaming, Twisted Vine, Hive Avenue, Taint Taint Taint, Matthew's Place through the Matthew Shepard Foundation, History Through Fiction, and Quarter Press. He's a former Peace Corps volunteer who served in Mauritania, West Africa. Originally from Central PA, he now lives in the Northside of Pittsburgh with his partner, cats, and birds.

http://michaellockett-author.com